Sirens screamed through the night.

Uncontrollable shudders shook her, and her legs quaked. For this one moment, Kayla allowed the strength and certainty of Rio's embrace to hold her up. She didn't refuse the comfort his arms gave her. His breathing and heartbeat were strong and reassuring under her left ear, and she pressed her head against his chest, her arms tight around his waist.

Rio's waist.

"You're okay, babe."

Babe.

The sanctity of their embrace evaporated as effectively as if Rio were a hypnotist and he'd snapped her out of a trance. A trance she couldn't afford to wander into, not if she was going to keep her emotions regarding him in check. It'd taken this long to finally accept that there was no hope for them.

This was the same man who'd hidden his identity from her. It paid to remember that.

* * *

We hope you enjoy the Silver Valley P.D. miniseries. Be sure to look for more stories in 2016!

If you're on Twitter, tell us what you think of Harlequin Romantic Suspense! #harlequinromsuspense

Dear Reader,

Weddings are usually a time of joy in Silver Valley, just like they are anywhere else. But when the mayor, who's suspected of criminal wrongdoing, ends up with a murdered assistant, it's enough to cast a pall on any event. I had fun writing about wedding planning amid such a terrible crime, and I hope you enjoy reading *Wedding Takedown*, SVPD #2.

I loved writing heroine Kayla Paruso, since her life *appears* so well-ordered, but after witnessing a murder she has to dig deep to help justice prevail, even though that involves her former lover, SVPD detective Rio Ortego. As Rio came to life on the page I discovered that he, too, was a more complex hero than first impressions might convey. Kayla and Rio are perfect for each other, but have to survive murder attempts and go through undercover training before they can begin to deal with their own emotional conflicts. Their chemistry is intense—these characters wanted me to write yet another love scene when they had a murderer to catch!

It's my wish that your time in Silver Valley is entertaining, and that you keep guessing who the killer is to the very end of the story.

Thank you so much for your continued support of my stories.

I'd love to connect with you. Please visit my website, www.gerikrotow.com, and sign up for my newsletter. Also find me at my author page on Facebook, Pinterest, Instagram and Twitter. Wherever you're comfortable chatting, I'm there!

Peace,

Geri

WEDDING TAKEDOWN

Geri Krotow

HARLEQUIN® ROMANTIC SUSPENSE

Recycling programs
for this product may
not exist in your area.

ISBN-13: 978-0-373-27981-4

Wedding Takedown

Copyright © 2016 by Geri Krotow

Printed in U.S.A.

™ www.Harlequin.com

Former naval intelligence officer and US Naval Academy graduate **Geri Krotow** draws inspiration from the global situations she's experienced. Geri loves to hear from her readers. You can email her via her website and blog, gerikrotow.com.

To Andrew Grey and Heidi Hormel,
Plotbusters Extraordinaire!

Chapter 1

"My order was very specific. I said absolutely no mums in the bouquet, and you sent an arrangement with three!"

Kayla Paruso knew that customer service was paramount to the success of Kayla's Blooms. That was the only thing that kept her smiling at Mrs. Vance, who came into the shop every week with a complaint. The elderly woman had been widowed only a year ago and Kayla figured if nitpicking about floral arrangements kept Mrs. Vance going, then so be it.

"I'm so sorry, Mrs. Vance. I'll send out a new arrangement tomorrow morning. Tell you what, I'll throw in a new vase for the inconvenience. Please pick one from that lower shelf and let me know what time you'd like the delivery."

"You know, in Europe it's considered bad luck to give mums. They're funeral flowers!" Mrs. Vance's dentures clicked as spittle flew from her mouth.

Poor thing.

"I didn't know that. Thanks for letting me know. Please do feel free to pick out a vase." How her voice stayed so upbeat was beyond her. Her older sister, Melody, had told her it was the way she'd spoken since childhood—always sounding as though she was excited and happy to see the person she was chatting with.

Mrs. Vance walked over to the shelf of vases, the heels of her stylish shoes tapping on the hardwood floor Kayla had sanded and re-stained two years ago, before she opened Kayla's Blooms. The lights were bright and her eyes were painfully dry after almost fifteen hours in the shop. It was time to call it a day.

"I'm glad you were here to deal with her." Jenny, her assistant, spoke quietly behind Kayla. Her hands flew as she pulled off florist paper and wrapped bouquet after bouquet of fresh flowers, finishing each with a colorful spring bow. The Passover and Easter holidays kept them working around the clock and Kayla was grateful for every order called in.

Even for Mrs. Vance.

"It's all part of the job, right? Besides, she did make it clear, no mums."

"That's my point. They weren't mums, not technically. They were asters. And she's never mistaken them for mums before."

"You're right. We have to give her some leeway. Her

daughter stopped in last week and told me she's thinking of placing Mrs. Vance in a memory care unit. The flowers looked like mums to her, and that's all that matters. It's no problem for us to make her up a new arrangement."

"Unless every other customer wants the same treatment."

"It's our policy to replace any unsatisfactory order, and that won't change." She wasn't going to try to explain to Jenny how hard and complicated the aging process could be, especially when dementia came into play. "Why don't you head home after you get these into the water buckets?"

"You don't have to tell me twice. What time do you need me tomorrow?"

"Eight o'clock is fine. I may be out on deliveries, but you can open the shop."

"I can come in earlier. You can't keep working at this pace."

"Don't worry about it. I need you fresh and chipper to face all the customers tomorrow. I thrive on this pace. My schedule isn't going to let up until after wedding season. This is why I got into this business—to keep moving."

"There's 'moving,' and there's the hamster wheel."

Kayla smiled but ignored Jenny's comment. Jenny was still in college, and spent three of her weekdays commuting to school, working for Kayla on the other two and filling in as needed. She was allowed to have her own opinion. It would be too easy to tell Jenny how much her life would change over the next few years. It was in those years that Kayla herself had realized she wanted to build a life with the permanence she'd never had as a child. Her childhood had been nomadic, spent moving around with her government-employed parents. Starting a new business had been a tremendous challenge but her patience had paid off, since the flower shop was all hers. And so far, it was operating at a profit.

Her cell phone vibrated in her apron pocket and she reached for it, her interest piqued when she saw the caller ID.

"Gloria, what can I do for you?" The Silver Valley mayor's wife, Gloria Charbonneau, was a new addition to her client list and could bring in an untold number of orders if she spread the word about Kayla's quality product. Kayla found the woman a bit high-strung, but couldn't really fault her—her husband had become mayor in a quickly thrown together election when the previous mayor of Silver Valley, a suburb of Harrisburg, PA, had been indicted for embezzlement.

And it was a charge that Kayla didn't believe one bit. She'd worked with Mayor Donner over the past two years and found her to be a locally grown politician who knew the area and its people, and did her best to get things done as needed. Amelia Donner was well-known in Silver Valley and many of the locals were still very upset at her sudden expulsion from office. Not to mention their wariness about the slick man who took her place, Tony Charbonneau. Mayor Donner had been a quintessential politician but she wasn't a criminal.

But apparently Kayla's opinion didn't stand up to the

courts that were still working to put the former mayor behind bars for her alleged crimes.

"This isn't about my usual order, Kayla. I need something bigger, and soon." Gloria Charbonneau's "usual" was a white centerpiece with seasonal flowers and a touch of color, depending upon the month and her mood. Replaced weekly, it was part of the standing-order list that was the backbone of Kayla's shop.

Last week's color choice had been black. Gloria preferred a contemporary style with a generous helping of gaudiness thrown in.

"Tell me what you need."

There was a long pause and when Gloria finally spoke it wasn't with her usual conviction.

"The mayor's, that is, *our* daughter is having a short-notice wedding. Next Saturday evening, at the Weddings and More Barn. Are you familiar with it?"

"Of course." Her older sister had used the venue three years ago, and her yoga friend Zora had mentioned it as a possibility for her upcoming wedding to an SVPD detective. The same guy Kayla had tried dating with no luck. Followed by another cop she was still trying to forget, months later. But Rio hadn't been just another cop, another date. They'd had something special, or so she'd thought. Until she'd realized how dangerous his job really was. She needed stability, not constant worry that her life's partner would be killed in a shoot-out.

Always the florist, never the bride.

And that was what she wanted, she reminded herself.

"Can you pull this off in a little more than a week?"

"That's what I do, Gloria." As she spoke soothingly to the woman known for her perfectionism, Kayla's mind raced with all that would need to be done between now and next Saturday. On top of the Easter weekend.

She'd be decorating a wedding as she ignored the sad state of her own love life.

"Cynthia doesn't know what she wants yet, in terms of a theme. I've asked my husband if his assistant can get some photos of the venue for me to use to brainstorm before I meet with you." Kayla wondered why Gloria wasn't using her own administrative assistant, whom Kayla had spoken to many times about floral deliveries.

"That sounds good, and if you don't get the photos before tomorrow, I have some of my own." She was grateful again for her nomadic childhood with parents in the United States Foreign Service. She'd learned early on that organization paid huge dividends during crunch times such as when they'd had to move across the globe to a new country and report to a new school, all within a week. And Cynthia Charbonneau's wedding was going to be the definition of *crunch*. "Why don't we meet sometime tomorrow and nail down the details?"

"I can come by your shop anytime."

"That'd be wonderful. Is eleven o'clock okay?"

"I'll see you then."

Kayla allowed herself a quick fist pump and a wink at Jenny.

"We just landed a wedding for next weekend."

"Do they want pastel eggs in the arrangements?"

Jenny held up one of the thousands of pale lavender, pink, yellow and blue floral picks she'd placed in arrangements over the past few days.

Kayla laughed.

"Probably not."

"I want this vase." Mrs. Vance held a large crystal-cut vase that she'd found on the top shelf. Kayla had all but forgotten about her sweet but persnickety customer.

"That's not one of the vases from my bouquet collection, Mrs. Vance."

"How much more will it cost me?"

Kayla didn't hesitate.

"Nothing. You've been so patient, I'll throw it in and have your new flowers out in the morning, sometime before ten o'clock. Does that work for you?"

Mrs. Vance beamed.

"Yes."

If only all of her customers could be made happy with a simple vase.

Kayla locked the shop's door almost an hour after Jenny left, two hours past closing time. The night air felt good on her cheeks. Warmer than inside, where she had to rely on refrigeration and air-conditioning to keep her stock fresh.

She was going to have to run into the Port of Baltimore to pick up flowers for the wedding next week. It might even have to be an extra drive added onto her usual pickup. Jenny couldn't do it due to her class schedule, and Kayla still hadn't hired a much-needed additional assistant. Soon, after the madness of the holiday weekend, she'd get on that.

She felt buoyed up as she calculated her revenue. Last year she'd feared the shop wouldn't last another six months, but the recession seemed to be lessening and people were still falling in love, getting married and dying. Funerals were a big part of her business and she appreciated the chance to be of comfort to grieving families and friends in their times of need.

Her florist van smelled of blooms and mud, a combination she loved. The van's purchase had been one of her smartest business decisions and she'd spared no expense, from the refrigerated back area to the up-to-date dashboard, which she used now to place a hands-free phone call.

"Hello?" Rob Owings, the owner of the Weddings and More Barn, answered on the first ring.

"Rob, sorry to bother you so late."

His chuckle made her smile.

"No such thing this time of year. Let me guess, it's about the Charbonneau wedding?"

"Yes. I still have the key from the Rotary dinner last week—"

"Sure, go on in and plan to your heart's content. I left the front lights on. Cynthia stopped by last weekend to check it out."

"Sounds like she was happy with it."

"I wasn't there when she checked it out. I had to give the key to Gloria to pass on to her. Gloria signed for the wedding when she returned the key."

"They're willing to pour a lot of money into a short-notice affair." She knew the deposit had to have been hefty for the three hundred guests they planned on.

"Yeah, I thought that was a little weird, but I'm not complaining." Rob had three kids, one in college, and had lost his wife to a drunk driver two years ago. Kayla had done the flowers for her funeral and also attended.

"I hear you. Thanks, and I'm sure we'll be talking more over the next week."

"You bet."

Instead of driving toward the small subdivision where she lived, she turned right and headed out of town, toward the farm fields that surrounded Silver Valley.

The moon was a crescent against the star-spangled night sky, the edge of sunset still on the western horizon. Kayla could get sucked into work and not step outside for hours on end, but deliveries and special events like this kept her out and about.

You're aiding the enemy.

A worm of guilt crept into her serenity and she let out an exasperated breath. Ever since last Christmas, when she'd delivered a bouquet of flowers to Zora, not realizing they were from a serial killer, her mind had been on overdrive. It was too easy to think that the rumors about the new mayor were true—that Tony Charbonneau was some kind of criminal who'd found a way to get rid of the previous mayor and get himself elected in short order. Even if the accusations against the previous mayor proved false, it didn't mean the new mayor was anything but lucky or extremely ambitious. Perhaps a bit of both.

And his wife had high-end tastes, which at times bordered on eccentric, usually in response to the most recent episode of her favorite reality TV series. She'd even send Kayla a video clip of one of the shows, demanding that her bouquets have the same shape. Kayla liked how her unique requests kept her on her artistic toes. It was easy to fall into the routine of everyday arrangements, and Kayla wanted to offer her customers something they couldn't find anywhere else.

The barn was dark but the LED light at the side entrance flooded the area as if it was daytime. Kayla was familiar with the building since she'd provided flowers for several weddings and graduations here over the past few years, first as a freelancer, taking contracts and storing flowers in her garage and kitchen refrigerator, and then after the shop opened, she'd been able to handle more volume.

The barn looked forlorn and dark in the spring night. Rob usually left a couple of lights on inside, on timers, but with his other job managing a dairy farm, he had his hands full. It was easy to let something small slip his mind. Kayla knew the feeling all too well.

Like how they'd put the most colorful aster blooms, normally more available in the fall, in Mrs. Vance's bouquet, when Kayla knew darn well that the woman would see them as plain old mums. She hadn't been expecting Mrs. Vance to label them harbingers of death, however.

Her van bounced up the worn path through the field beside the large white barn and she winced as she hit a deep rut. She pulled off the muddy path and onto a dry patch of dirt. Better to walk a few hundred yards to the barn than risk wrecking her van in the dark. Spring thaw had a way of turning the hard clay soil of South Central Pennsylvania into thick, sucking mud not dissimilar to the mud fields she'd seen in the Netherlands as a child. Back when Dad had worked at the Hague and Mom had taken long hours away from her job as a private contractor to take Kayla and her siblings, Melody and Keith, on long sojourns through Europe.

Her favorite had been in the tulip-growing region of the Netherlands. Holland had opened her nose and her eyes to the brilliance of bulb flowers, from hyacinths to parrot tulips. She hadn't been happy as a child unless there was dirt under her nails from helping her mother plant rows and rows of bulbs, seeds and rose bushes.

Her parents had indulged her when she proclaimed she was going to be a florist and own her own shop. They'd breathed an audible sigh of relief when she'd been accepted to Penn State and majored in horticulture. They assumed she'd end up in research.

Instead her passion for dirt and flowers grew. But rather than being streamlined like a standard Dutch tulip, she'd behaved like the sprawling parrot tulip with its petals falling haphazardly, spreading her interests into the cultivation of hybrids while running her own florist shop and design studio.

As she killed the engine, she thought she heard something high-pitched above the regular shutting-down noises. She paused. The van was only eighteen months old and she was *so* not in the mood for it to be in need of repair. She prayed the rut hadn't ruined her front-end alignment or jiggled anything else loose.

Forcing away the annoying thoughts, she got out and her feet immediately sank into the squishy mud. Her bright fuchsia rain boots kept her feet warm and dry.

She clomped through the mud, selecting the key to the barn by feel from her key ring. It had a large soft cushiony frame around the top. She walked past a sedan and wondered if someone else was here.

"No! You can't do this—" A woman's voice, loud and strident.

A gunshot, punctuated by a woman's scream, sounded in the still night, rooting Kayla to the spot.

She *had* heard something high-pitched a few moments ago. Screaming.

The sound of items crashing inside the barn unfroze her feet and her mind with them. The van was too far away for her to make it there, start the engine and drive off before whoever had fired the gun would know she was there.

Call the police.

She ran to the side of the barn, ducking low from the view of the side door. The door's window glowed with the kitchen's bright fluorescent lights. She made out the bulky figure of a man through the slatted blinds but couldn't risk taking a closer look. Not if she was going to be of any help to the woman whose screaming she'd heard.

That gunshot and scream hadn't been like in the movies. It was real, scary as hell, and she knew she could be on the receiving end of a bullet if she didn't play this right.

Crawling on her knees to avoid detection, she squeezed between a tractor pull and a pile of hay bales. She worried that her van was too far down the drive and too much in plain view of anyone who left via the driveway. Did the shooter own the car she'd walked by?

She wanted to run for it and drive away but she couldn't risk the noise of her engine starting. Her logo was emblazoned on the van, making an anonymous getaway impossible. It would be a siren call to whoever had fired that shot to come after her, too.

Shivers wracked her. From shock or an adrenaline rush, she had no idea as she hunkered down and willed herself to be one with the damp squishy ground and prickly hay bales. She pulled her phone out of her pocket and quickly dialed 911.

Chapter 2

Detective Riordan Ortega pressed the gas pedal to the floor as he sped along the farm road that led to the Weddings and More Barn. Rio wanted to get to the call before the other SVPD units made it.

He liked to be the first on the scene to any major crime in town. It had nothing to do with who'd called in the gunshot, and everything to do with his instinctual sense of the ticking clock when it came to crime. The sooner he got the investigation under way, the better chance of catching the culprit.

Silver Valley had always had its share of crime but lately things had been different—busier than he'd ever experienced since joining SVPD a decade ago. They'd just wrapped up the "Female Preacher Killer" case last December, only to be involved full-time in the embezzlement case against the former mayor. Tying up the loose ends on three murders by the serial killer had occupied all his time, and he'd been grateful that the Treasury Department had come into play for the mayor's case. Because of the embezzlement charges and large amounts of money at stake, the Secret Service had been alerted and then pulled in their former boss, the US Department of Treasury. Secret Service was under Homeland Security these days but Rio still worked with many of the agents he'd met when he'd started on SVPD. Rio loved his job and knew he was good at it, but making sense out of columns of numbers wasn't something that turned him on.

Unlike Kayla Paruso.

Shit. *Kayla.*

She'd called in the emergency. A shoot-out right now, so close to the mayor's daughter's wedding, was too suspicious for Rio. Mayor Charbonneau and his gang of thugs were trouble, and had been since they'd arrived in town, coincidentally at the same time as the newest Silver Valley residents, who were trying to set up a cult on the outskirts of town. Rio didn't believe in coincidences, not when it came to criminal behavior.

"What's your ETA, Rio?" The dispatcher spoke in his ear.

"Two minutes, tops. Anything new?"

"Caller isn't talking. She's kept the line open and we're hearing shouts."

Mother of God, please let her be okay. Keep Kayla safe.

The first time he'd seen her she was delivering a

bunch of flowers to the station for one of the female cops. He couldn't remember a thing about the delivery except for Kayla's huge blue eyes and golden blond hair. And the way her black tights had displayed her long legs and perfect full ass. He'd imagined the breasts hidden by her jean jacket as full and luscious, and he hadn't been disappointed when they'd made love on the one occasion he'd ignored his personal credo to remain unencumbered. He'd stopped by her flower shop and asked her out. And taken her to his bed, in his torn-apart home on the edges of town.

He'd since finished the renovations on the house, one a Realtor friend of his had stumbled upon three years ago. It was perfect for a flipper but after pouring his sweat and blood into the hardwood floors, he'd decided to keep the single-story rambler on the edge of one of Silver Valley's farm fields.

He'd imagined taking Kayla there after he'd finished it, when the dust had settled and it was a proper home. He wanted to show her he wasn't a complete jerk who dated women only for sex. That he wasn't going to be the guy who loved her and left her. Because it hadn't been "only" sex with Kayla. But she'd been long gone and they'd been long over before he ever had the chance to bring her home again.

Kayla.

The lack of information from the dispatcher annoyed him.

"Anything new?"

"Nothing, Rio."

"Has she tried to text anything?"

"No, we told her to sit tight and stay quiet until re-sponders arrive."

"How close are the other units?"

"Patrol two-three-three is five minutes out."

"Where the hell were they?" At this rate none of them would be there in enough time to save anyone.

The taste of bile rose in the back of his throat and he cursed.

"What's that, Rio?"

"Nothing."

He had to keep it together. Nothing had ever dis-tracted him from his life's purpose: serving the public. He'd known he wanted to be a police officer since he was eight years old, when his uncle Jimmy had given him a tour of the station in Harrisburg and he'd fallen in love with the way the police department employees had laughed and joked with each other as though the job was nothing but fun.

Only later, as a rookie, had he learned why they really joked with each other. It was to alleviate the deep sense of duty that sometimes weighed unbearably heavy because of the brutal realities of their jobs. The violence, the senseless killings. The gore.

Not Kayla. Not on his watch.

The phone lay muted on top of the hale bay next to her, the screen turned off to prevent anyone from seeing her. Some reptilian part of her brain shouted at Kayla to slither under the bales and simply hide until the police arrived.

Where was Keith when she needed his savvy?

She prayed that she could somehow channel her brother's firefighting survival instinct. Because things weren't getting any quieter inside the barn and she needed some kind of crime-scene smarts.

Rio would be the best help here.

She gave herself a quick, silent shake in the darkness. This wasn't the time to revisit that hurt.

Stay alive.

Kayla knew better than to go inside and try to help whoever was struggling with the owner of the low voice. From what she could gather it was one man and one woman and they weren't talking about anything pleasant.

But the woman's voice had gotten quieter since the gunshot. Maybe the shot hadn't been intended to hurt anyone, and this was some kind of crazy domestic argument. Kayla heard the woman's humming voice as she spoke to the angry man. The man's voice conveyed a fury that had Kayla quaking.

Kayla wondered if she was crazy. Maybe it wasn't a gunshot she'd heard, but something else, maybe a piece of furniture overturning.

She rested against the barn wall, behind the stacked bales. It was wet and cold and smelled of alfalfa. The one plant on the entire planet that Kayla was allergic to. She wasn't worried about her watery eyes or itchy nose, though. Not yet.

First, she needed to survive whatever was going on, and hoped it wasn't anything more than her overactive imagination.

The door shook as a heavy object hit it, followed

by the creak of the hinges and a loud slamming. Kayla moved slowly, needing to see what was happening. As she peered between two bales, she made out the open door. It was a yawning black hole, indicating the lights had been turned off.

Shuffling, a grunt or two, crying. Soft, pain-filled crying.

"Help me, someone." The low, raspy plea reached her ears and it felt as though Kayla was as injured as the woman. If there was any way she could help her…

Kayla stood up from her crouch and looked over the stack of bales. A prone figure lay in the walkway, a woman. The harsh glare of the overhead security lights illuminated dark hair and a business outfit—skirt and jacket. On her stomach, she leaned on her forearms as if she was in a yoga sphinx pose. Kayla immediately recognized her. Scanning the entire area as much as it was feasible while behind the bales, she didn't see anyone else. The man must have left.

"Meredith!" she whispered as loudly as possible.

"Help. Me."

Kayla rose to do just that when a shot rang through the night, and Meredith's head slammed into the ground.

Oh no.

Kayla pressed against the hay, her heartbeat and the ringing from the gunshot loud in her ears. She didn't know if she was hidden from the killer or if she needed to make a run for it.

She'd never outrun a bullet.

The sound of approaching footsteps was quickly followed by the sound of something scraping and a grunt. A loud *thwack* as an object hit the ground. Peering through the hay bale, she could only see Meredith's hands, still as her head lay between them, a briefcase with file folders splayed in front of her where a dark spot grew into a larger circle. Blood. She wished the side light of the barn door wasn't so bright—the image of Meredith bleeding out would be burned into Kayla's mind.

Someone cleared his or her throat. She heard the distinct sound of a zipper and then the sound of liquid hitting the side of the barn.

The killer was taking a leak?

"It's done. I'll see you in the morning."

The sound of the deep voice, obviously making a phone call, startled Kayla and she stumbled, landing on the damp ground with a soft thud.

"Who's there?"

The harsh voice matched the throat clearing, the furious man she'd heard before. She was in trouble. Kayla crawled on her belly around to the other side of the bales and without stopping rose to her feet and ran for her life.

Rio's headlights illuminated the open side door of the barn and the figure in front of it. He saw a dark shape darting toward the back of the barn as he got out of his vehicle. As he chased the assailant, weapon drawn, the figure blended into the darkness that surrounded the barn. Rio swore under his breath and tapped the microphone on his communication gear.

"Suspect ran into the fields behind the barn. Do we have units on the other side of the woods? I'm turning back to investigate a possible victim near the east side door."

"Roger that, Rio."

"Send a unit to Waverly Street to intercept possible escape." Waverly bisected the wooded area the dark figure had vanished into.

Heading back to the barn, he let out a silent thank-you that the female lying outside wasn't Kayla—the hair was too dark, the woman too tall. As he drew closer he saw that not only was she facedown, but she'd also been shot in the back of the head. Blood stained the ground around her head in a black halo. He kneeled to feel for a carotid pulse. The entire left side of her head was gone.

Muttering another oath, he searched for the pulse just in case. Just in case the blood and torn flesh looked worse than the real injury.

Unfortunately, his initial assessment was correct. As he expected, there was no pulse.

"I've got a dead female, probable homicide. Call in forensics and the coroner."

"Have you located the caller yet, Rio?"

"No joy. Still looking." His gaze landed on her van. "Going to investigate her van."

"Do not go into the van or barn without backup, sir."

What the dispatcher was telling him was standard protocol. But Kayla could be in either place, bleeding out. He couldn't stand on protocol.

"Kayla!" He called over and over, pulling open the doors of her van as he searched for any sign of her.

Nothing.

Her phone.

He directed his frustration at dispatch. "She still on the line?"

"The line's still open but there hasn't been any communication since about seven minutes ago."

It felt as if he'd been on the case for days instead of ten minutes. But time was never reliable during the heat of a crime. Judging from how warm the victim's body was, she'd been breathing just minutes earlier.

"Has anyone intercepted the suspect?"

"No, but local residents in the neighboring subdivision report someone running through their yards, alerting dogs. One caller saw someone dressed in black get into a late-model sedan and drive away."

"Did they get plates?"

"No. We've got a sheriff's chopper inbound."

A single assailant so far. Either he'd shot Kayla, too, and she was on the ground nearby, or she was still hiding, worried for her life.

"Kayla!" He ran back to the barn and entered the kitchen, flipping on the light switch next to the door. The commercial illumination revealed a scene of total chaos. Pots and pans of all sizes were everywhere. A butcher block had been knocked over and several chef knives were strewn over the tiled floor. One knife lay closest to the door, blood on it.

"Kayla!"

"I'm here."

He spun around, weapon drawn, his aim steady.

"It's me, Rio. Kayla. Or don't you remember?"

Slowly he lowered his gun and allowed his arms to

drop to his sides. Never had the sight of someone been so welcome. A charge of hot attraction went from his heart to his dick, and if there wasn't a dead body that needed tending to outside of the kitchen they stood in, he knew he'd have her in his arms and laying across the prep table, naked, in a minute flat. So much for his professional pride.

"Kayla."

He saw the wariness in her eyes. Not fear from the shock of what she'd just been through, but what he'd put there when he'd never called her back after she told him she couldn't see him anymore.

Even that wasn't enough to keep her from catapulting herself into his arms, forcing him to take a step back. His butt hit the edge of the prep table as his arms went around her, and he felt a sudden flash of regret that they weren't here as lovers, instead of as a murder witness and cop.

Chapter 3

Sirens screamed through the night as uncontrollable shudders shook her shoulders and made her legs quake. For just this moment, she allowed the strength and certainty of Rio's embrace to hold her up as they stood outside, waiting. She didn't refuse the comfort his arms gave. His heartbeat was strong and reassuring under her left ear. She pressed her head harder against his chest, her arms tight around his waist.

Rio's waist.

"You're okay, babe."

Babe.

The cocoon of their embrace evaporated as effectively as if Rio was a hypnotist and he'd snapped her out of a trance. A trance she couldn't afford to wander into, not if she was going to keep her emotions regarding Rio in check. It'd taken this long to finally accept there was no hope for them. This was the same man who went undercover, whose life was at risk each and every day he went to work. Definitely not the kind of man she envisioned herself with for the long run.

"I'm okay. But she's not, is she? Is she dead, Rio?"

"Yes, she's dead. Do you know who it is, Kayla?"

She blinked. Rio was every inch the cop. She knew more than ever what mattered most to Rio. Being a detective.

"Yes, I know her. Knew her. But not personally. I mean, not well. She was in our yoga class until she had to quit because she'd taken on this job with the mayor. It was going to be her big break into politics. She was so young, Rio, so alive. She was asking, begging for help. And I couldn't do anything…" She didn't finish, didn't have to as she looked at the body of the woman, facedown and forever still.

"Did you catch a look at who did this to her?"

"Only a glimpse. Mostly I heard him. Big, booming deep voice. He was really angry from the sounds of it. I heard her scream. Then a gunshot—the first shot was while they were still inside the barn. As I got closer I heard her talking. She was speaking low, probably trying to convince him not to hurt her. After he threw her out here, she asked me for help, Rio. She was still alive, but the second shot killed her." Her insides turned bilious as she recounted the horror. "I'm sorry." She turned and tried to run but ended up on her knees at the side of the barn door, retching. Rio kept his hand on her back, between her shoulder blades. The reassurance in such a simple gesture was immeasurable. She soaked up his energy, hoping it would soothe her heaving stomach.

Facing him again, she tried to look anywhere but at Meredith. "I'm sorry."

"Nothing to apologize for." His eyes were dark and unreadable.

"You've never barfed at a scene, I'll bet."

"You'd be surprised." Gently he led her off to the side, away from Meredith's still form. "Keep telling me what you remember, Kayla."

"Okay." She clasped her hands in front of her. If only she'd come tomorrow morning, instead...

"Did he see you or your van?"

"No, I don't think so. The van's too far down the drive and he didn't come outside until after he threw her out here. He heard me and asked 'Who's there?' He knew I was out here, heard me, but you showed up and spooked him. I made it look like I was running into the darkness around the woods, but then I doubled back and hid behind one of the buildings next to the barn. Right after I heard sirens and then saw the lights from what must have been your car, I saw him run past, not looking for anyone, from what I could tell. When he took off for the woods, I went inside."

Thank God.

"It might have been me, but probably it was the sirens scared him away." Rio paused. "Any chance it was a woman with a deep voice?"

She shook her head.

"No, I don't think so. It definitely sounded like a

man and he had heavy footsteps. The silhouette was masculine, large. I heard him urinate against the side of the building. And he'd started to pull apart the pile of hay bales where I was hiding. Most women can't lift a bale and toss it as quickly as he did. If I hadn't made a run for it, or you hadn't shown up, he'd have seen me within seconds."

Rio's expression remained neutral except for the compassionate light in his eyes. A light she'd once thought he might be able to focus on her for more than a round of mind-blowing sex, a light that might warm her long past the early heat they'd shared. But Rio was a cop, from the top of his raven hair to the bottom of his sexy feet—which she'd noticed on the few occasions she'd seen him naked. He had limitless compassion, for victims and the community he protected. There wasn't any room for personal relationships in Rio's world. And no room for understanding her need to have a man with a more stable profession in her life.

She'd tried dating a cop, another SVPD detective, before Rio and it didn't work out, either. Of course, now that same cop was engaged to her friend Zora, so the reality was that when things were supposed to work, they did.

She and Rio weren't supposed to work.

As soon as she'd found out Rio was a cop, she'd felt the warning tugs from her heart but ignored them. Because she and Rio had shared a chemistry she'd never experienced before. But in the cold mornings after they'd made love, she'd had to get honest with herself. She couldn't take the chance of a future full of loss due to Rio's profession. Once she'd found out he'd been assigned to work her brother's case, she'd used that fact to call off their brief relationship.

"If it hadn't been me, someone from SVPD would have been here. We weren't going to let you get hurt." Rio's confident tone was another one of his professional tools. She didn't disagree with him, but she acknowledged that if the killer had decided to shoot through the hay, she might be lying here as dead as Meredith, who was sprawled in the mud path with her briefcase in front of her and all her pretty floral files spilled out in a haphazard fan. Organization didn't matter in death.

"Detective Ortega, we've got some footprints out behind the barn and Officer Pasczenko found two shells." A fresh-faced police officer stood next to them, his eagerness to get the job done reassuring in the dark night.

"Tell the forensics teams. They'll be here soon if they aren't already."

"You want *me* to tell them, Detective?"

"That's what I said, Officer Ogden."

"Yes, sir."

The officer's obvious pride at being trusted to complete the communication would have been heartwarming if Kayla wasn't frozen in shock.

"This was supposed to be a simple trip to do some preplanning for a wedding."

"Whose wedding?"

"Cynthia Charbonneau. The mayor's daughter. She's planning a last-minute ceremony for next weekend. Her mother called and offered me a generous retainer fee for the extra work it's going to take. I couldn't turn her down, even in the middle of the spring rush."

"Would you have otherwise?"

"Turned her down? No, I don't base my business on rumors about my clients. And she's been a good regular customer—she has a standing order for a fresh arrangement each week."

Rio's silence conveyed his agreement. Damn it, but she wished she wasn't still so in tune with him. That she didn't notice that in his black T-shirt and the casual blazer he looked like some kind of freaking model.

It would be much easier if Rio looked like a toad.

But even if he looked like the ugliest creature on earth, she'd still have a problem. Because Rio Ortega was the most loving, most generous man she'd ever met.

He was also the most career-driven—at times arrogant but always professional—law-enforcement worker she'd ever known. And she'd known plenty.

"Do you think it's true, Rio? Do you think the mayor rigged the election?"

"I can't comment on that, Kayla. But what I can say is that if it smells like manure, chances are that's what it is. No matter how pretty the field it's in."

"You're never short on your own kind of poetry, Rio."

"You should have stuck around, Kayla. I could have regaled you with all kinds of fancy words."

The heat in her cheeks was immediate, as was her desire to close the short distance between them and press her body against his. But anger reined her in as she realized that was his intent—to remind her of the hot nights they'd spent together when she'd agreed to date him late last fall.

Before he'd told her he was a cop. A detective. His not telling her about his career was what she'd used as her defense against his potent invitation to take their relationship deeper. She'd argued that she couldn't be with a man who wouldn't reveal who he was or what he did right from the get-go. The mere thought of being with someone who went undercover for unknown lengths of time stressed her out.

And admittedly she still felt a little stupid for not facing her trepidations about his profession before she'd gone to bed with him, much less started to fall for him.

"I'm sorry, Kayla. You've just had a terrible shock and I'm giving you grief. We're going to have to continue this at the station—I need your statement. Do you mind going with Officer Ogden and getting started? You don't need to be out here in the cold any longer. I'll be along shortly."

"I can drive myself." She needed the reassurance of her van. It was a second office, and a reminder that she wasn't just an almost-victim of a crime, or a murder witness.

"Let Officer Ogden drive you. I'll have another officer bring your van to the station."

The real Rio was back, the one with whom she could get herself into a lot of trouble. His hand was on her elbow, his warmth soothing.

"I'm all right, honest. I'll follow Officer Ogden there."

"It's not a question, Kayla. It's protocol. You were at the scene of a murder. We have to take a look at the van before you get back into it."

"You're kidding, right? You're treating me like a suspect?"

Rio's mouth was a thin line. "Damn it, Kayla, I know you're not a murderer. But I can't make any exceptions—"

"When it comes to your job. I think this is right about where we left off last year, isn't it?"

She wrenched away her arm and stalked over to Officer Ogden, who stood next to a Silver Valley PD sedan. Kayla had no idea why or how it had happened, but she'd found herself at the mercy of the law again.

Rio watched as Kayla got into the patrol car with Ogden. Forensics would do a formal check of her van later.

He'd learned through years of police work to never rely on just his eyes. The criminal could have had an accomplice or circled back and hidden in the roomy van. Kayla hadn't thought of that—she'd only recognized that he needed to be scrupulous about inspecting her van. He saw it all the time—witnesses and victims felt as if they were being victimized a second time by the work the police needed to do to ensure justice prevailed.

It stung more than usual because the witness was Kayla. He'd relived those few weeks with her more than he'd ever admit to himself, always questioning whether they still might be together if he had told her from the beginning what he did and what case he was working on.

He hadn't expected to have those feelings after that first night. But when one night turned into a week, he'd had to tell her that he didn't work only as a detective. He often went undercover. She hadn't been happy to find that out. When her brother's case came up, he could have passed it to another detective, could have done a lot of things to preserve at least their friendship.

But she found out first, when she'd been in the same diner as Rio. He'd been eating a quick lunch with three uniformed officers. As a detective he almost always wore civilian clothes, his weapon holstered under a jacket or blazer. That day he'd finished up a long undercover case and was still dressed to fit in with the members of the drug ring he'd infiltrated. Baggy jeans, big gold jewelry and his baseball cap on backward. The warmth and rush of awareness he associated with Kayla had hit him when he'd looked across the booths and found Kayla staring at him. She'd been dining with her girlfriend from yoga class Zora Krasny.

The "oh, shit" moment had been the end of their relationship.

She wouldn't even look at him now as she sat in the police car, staring straight ahead through the window.

Kayla's pallor shook him more than he cared to admit. The woman he'd thought he might be falling for was strong and quick to defend anyone, from her employees to a surly customer.

Her defense of herself had been pretty good, too. When she'd found out what his line of work was, any hope of a future with Kayla was crushed under the iron will she employed to break up with him and keep him out of her life. The stress of finding out that her brother, a local firefighting hero recently promoted to chief, was being charged with negligence at his job didn't help matters. It wasn't just that, though. According to her brother, Keith, the real issue was her need for control over her life,

Still, it would have been nice to be the man who'd changed her mind about what she needed. He'd like to be the man who changed her mind about a lot of things, and those included allowing a man to treat her well and to love her the way she deserved.

He pulled on one of the many pairs of latex gloves he kept in his pocket as he walked over to the crime scene. He silently accepted the wallet one of the forensic team members handed him.

"We found it in the kitchen. Everything was spilled out of her purse." Officer Kaufmann was a seasoned forensics expert on SVPD and one Rio enjoyed working with because he always shot straight from the hip.

"Meredith Houseman." He scrutinized her driver's license photo. The name was familiar and when he looked at her body, the business suit, there was no doubt she was the woman Kayla had mentioned earlier.

"The mayor's executive assistant."

"Yes, sir. Should we call him?"

"Hell no, not yet. Let's leave that to Superintendent Todd." Rio didn't want the mayor or any of his cronies nosing around his murder investigation. Not now, not at all. He still wasn't convinced that Mayor Charbonneau was more than a front for the recently reformed cult that was trying to set up shop on the outskirts of Silver Valley. The embezzlement charges against the previous mayor had happened too quickly, too conveniently as far as Rio was concerned. And Mayor Charbonneau's appearance in Silver Valley just in time for the special election had been suspicious.

And now the newly elected mayor's assistant was dead. Murdered at the same place where the mayor's daughter was supposed to be getting married in a little more than a week.

"Detective Ortega? We've found something unusual on the body." The county coroner stood in front of him, his normally quiet demeanor agitated.

"What's that?"

"It looks like her ribs were smashed in, probably collapsing at least one lung. She took a brutal beating before she was shot."

"Damn it."

Chapter 4

"Rio, you and I both know that while the rumors may prove correct, unless we have evidence of wrongdoing, we can't ask for a search warrant on the new mayor's residence. No can do." Colt Todd, Silver Valley's superintendent of police, leveled his cool gaze on Rio. There was no sense in arguing with him.

"Yes, sir."

"We can't afford to do anything less than what's perfectly legal and appropriate throughout this investigation. Is that clear?"

"Yes, sir." Rio couldn't argue with his boss, not on this one. SVPD had plenty going on at the moment, between providing testimony to put a serial killer behind bars for life, keeping an eye on a cult from New York that was trying to reunite in their jurisdiction and investigating the validity of the evidence they'd collected against the former mayor. Of course, Rio didn't think for one minute that their former mayor had been involved in any of the charges against her. It was a setup, and he'd bet his last dollar that the new mayor was at least peripherally involved, if not behind the entire scheme.

"Do you have any leads on the victim?" Todd's face had its usual neutral expression, but Rio heard the weariness in his tone. SVPD was being slammed from all sides by crimes that, while they looked unrelated, were proving to be linked in damning ways. The major connection was to the former cult members, all convicted felons. SVPD had to have proof to request restraining orders, or to force these suspicious new citizens of Silver Valley to leave by having the state rescind its permission to allow them to serve probation in Pennsylvania instead of New York.

"I have a few leads, sir. Two officers are out now, informing the victim's parents. The victim is Meredith Houseman, age twenty-seven, Silver Valley resident. A graduate of Mount St. Mary's College in Maryland. She had a degree in political science. She worked as a political intern in DC and here in Harrisburg before landing the job with Mayor Charbonneau. She was living at home with her parents while she earned money to go to law school—she'd been accepted by Penn State to study at Dickinson."

"Damn shame." Colt Todd shook his head, his frown deepening to a scowl. "There's going to be a huge backlash with this, especially the media. They're still not satisfied Charbonneau got into office legally."

Neither was Rio, and he suspected his boss agreed, but it wasn't anything they verbalized. It didn't matter, not until they found solid evidence that the new mayor was behind any illegal doings. SVPD wasn't a small department, with thirty officers and two to three detectives depending upon operational tempo. It was considered midsize and was usually more than enough to serve the twenty thousand citizens of Silver Valley.

"Debbie's on it, sir." Rio referred to the SVPD's spokesperson. She'd moved up from her job as receptionist when the Female Preacher Killer had been in the middle of his killing spree, wreaking havoc on Silver Valley last Christmas.

"Great. One more thing, Rio. You'd better sit down for this."

Here it comes.

"You understand that you have to consider Kayla Paruso as a suspect. And then, once you clear her, we need to keep an eye on her. Make sure she's safe."

"She isn't a killer, sir."

Todd held up his hands. "For legal purposes, Rio. I know damn well she's not a criminal, much less a murderer. But this is the second murder investigation she's involved in, and she is the only witness to this one. We have no other leads and I will not have the DA or governor coming after SVPD for anything procedurally imperfect."

"Yes, sir."

"Stop placating me, Rio. Do all of the usual workups you'd do on any other suspect. It won't be as heavy a workload since you did a preliminary investigation on her after she delivered those flowers to Zora Krasny last Christmas. For all we know the crazy cult might be trying to get to her next." He referred to the bouquet of flowers a serial killer had sent to the person he'd hoped would be a future victim via Kayla's floral shop. But Zora had been working undercover with fellow SVPD detective Bryce Campbell to lure the criminal out. The case had gotten larger than expected when Zora's biological mother, a member of a cult Zora had helped break up when she escaped as a child, showed up in Silver Valley. The same cult members were being released from prison and were settling in a trailer park on the outskirts of town.

"Sir, we both know she's not a suspect. Not really. And her involvement with the potential cult is nil. On a personal note, I know her—knew her—well. She's a good person, boss."

Colt searched his face and a slow grin cracked his usual tough expression. "Nice to know you have at least some kind of a personal life, Rio. Nevertheless, we both know how important it is to keep our paperwork in order. Since you don't think she's culpable, there isn't any conflict of interest as far as I'm concerned." Colt Todd leaned forward and rubbed his temples before he opened his eyes.

"The cult nonsense isn't going to go away quickly or quietly. We're dealing with some very determined people who will do anything to gain a foothold of power in a place like Silver Valley. We have everything they'd want—access to major East Coast highways, proximity to New York, Philadelphia, Baltimore and DC. We have good people here for the most part. But the heroin dealers and counterfeiters are taking their toll."

"We're going to beat them, too, boss."

"Yes, we are. We may need some help along the way, though."

"We already have FBI and Treasury working in our area, sir." Rio had no issues with the Feds and had, in fact, made several good contacts with agents operating locally. It was a mutually beneficial exchange of information and they all wanted the same thing: to put the bad guys behind bars and keep them the hell out of Silver Valley. "You're talking about the Trail Hikers?"

"Yeah."

Rio was familiar with the Trail Hikers, a government shadow agency that contracted agents who worked undercover, not only in Silver Valley and the Harrisburg area, but also throughout the United States as needed.

"I'm not full-time TH, sir, but I've been cleared to operate with them, and I received the introductory training. I'm aware of what they're capable of. But I don't think we're in that much of a bind yet."

"I didn't think we were, either, but without their help we would have never brought down the Female Preacher Killer in time. We might still be chasing that bastard."

"Sir, we'll get Meredith's killer, too. He's amateur at best, to have confronted the mayor's personal assistant in a place where anyone could have walked in at any time. Chances are it's someone the mayor knows." He wanted to wrap this up with Todd. Kayla was somewhere in the building, waiting to give her statement. But Colt wasn't done with him.

"Watch it, Rio. We can't start operating on assumptions. We both know where that will get us. I'm asking you to keep an open mind. If you see anyone you think is a Trail Hiker, you can't let them know you suspect there's a bigger investigation afoot. It's for all of our safety."

"Keep my eyes open and my mouth shut. I know the routine, boss."

That got a full grin out of Colt Todd, a rarity when his boss was stressed.

As Rio let himself out of his superior's office, he couldn't shake the feeling that it might be the last smile he'd see from his boss in a long time.

Colt Todd watched Rio depart as an attractive silver-haired woman walked into his office.

"Claudia. You're working late. Nice to see you."

"Colt. I heard about the murder." She shut the door behind her. When she turned back to him, she held out her hand. They shook and not for the first time he wished he could tug on her slim but strong arm and bring her up against him, lower his mouth to hers and…

"I trust I'm not interrupting you?" She motioned to the door Rio had just exited.

"Only our most recent murder investigation. Please, sit down." He waited until she slid into the chair before he lowered himself into his. "It's damn vexing, Claudia. When I was a rookie, we were pressed if we had one or two murders a decade. Now we've had more in the past six months than the last five years. What the hell is going on with this town?"

"I think we both suspect the same thing, Colt."

"I can't wait to take down these cult maniacs."

"That's what I'm here for. I have to ask you, and the SVPD, to give the True Believers a wide berth."

"What do you mean by that?" He already knew, but he wasn't going to let her off the hook, no matter how damn attractive she was.

"Higher levels of government are interested in the cult, Colt. How it's reorganizing, why it's picked Silver Valley and if Leonard Wise is back in town." She named the original leader of the cult, a man who had created a colony of children with young women convinced they had to listen to him. "I can't say much more, except that we need to monitor them. They may lead to some bigger crooks. And a bigger scheme than taking over a town of twenty thousand in suburban Pennsylvania."

He looked at her and admired how she didn't blink, didn't flinch, as he'd been known to make many cops, and especially criminals, do. "You're asking me to keep the residents of Silver Valley in danger from these crazies and to put my force at risk for longer than necessary, Claudia."

"Yes, I am. And it's not a request, Colt, so your conscience can be clear. It's an order from way above my pay grade." Claudia was a retired United States Marine Corps general. "Above her pay grade" referred to the highest levels of government.

"If it has the attention of the White House, why not bring in more FBI?"

"Trail Hikers are elite, Colt. The FBI is fantastic at what it does. But we don't know how far the cult's reach is. Who's really calling the shots. Leonard Wise could be a front man for someone, something else. Until we have more concrete answers we can't call in anything that would arouse suspicion."

"Or spook the cult away."

Claudia nodded. "You got it. I hate it as much as you that Silver Valley has become the petri dish to observe these slime bags. All I can do is promise that TH is here, backing up SVPD whether or not your officers are aware of it."

"How much support will we get from your group?" He knew he had Claudia's support as the group CEO, but even she had superiors to answer to.

"As much as you need, like always. As long as our budget holds out, which, trust me, it will." She shifted forward in her seat. "Can you fill me in on what you have on the Houseman murder? Rio will file a report for us, but I want to hear it from you first."

"You must think the murder's related to the cult, Claudia. Or is there something more I don't know?"

"No, I have no connections. Yet. But a mayor voted into office in such a rush, especially a political thug whose specialty until now has been New Jersey politics, raises red flags. We can't rule out the True Believers manipulating local politics for their own gain."

"You're leaving something out, Claudia, but I'll play along." He waited for her to smile and felt a rush of warmth to his crotch that he had to admit was a damned welcome feeling after years of living his self-imposed celibate lifestyle since his wife had died eight years ago.

Maggie. God, he still missed her. But when Claudia was around, the pain diminished. He filled her in on what he knew.

"Kayla Paruso, the florist from last Christmas who delivered the message in a bouquet to Zora Krasny." Claudia wasn't asking, she was thinking aloud. The woman had a steel trap for a brain. Another reason he was attracted to her. "We did an extensive background check on her at the time. She was raised by Foreign Service officers and has lived globally, probably conversational in two if not three languages besides English."

"That's not going to help us solve this, Claudia. She barely caught a look at the guy and describes his voice as deep and masculine."

"From a polyglot that's not a bad thing. I'm sure she'd be able to identify the voice again, in court. What I'm more interested in is her potential as a Trail Hiker." Claudia's eyes gleamed and the color on her high cheekbones conveyed her enthusiasm at adding to her team of super-trained law-enforcement agents.

"A florist? Claudia, I'm a simple man, the leader of a team of local cops. But even I know the importance of having the training and background to go into any kind of law enforcement. I doubt Kayla Paruso knows the difference between a pistol and a rifle."

"Because she's a woman?"

"Hell no. Because she's an artistic type. Have you met her? She's a pretty woman, very intelligent and very focused on her flower shop. It's her life."

"That kind of focus can easily translate into what we need on TH, especially for undercover surveillance." Claudia's eyes narrowed. Colt hid his amusement because he didn't want Claudia to think he was making fun of her. He wasn't. He was thrilled that he could make her react like this. It brought him back to his first thoughts about Claudia when she'd walked into the office…

"Don't, Colt." Her gaze was steady, her voice calm, but he saw the tremor in her hands. "I know what you're thinking and it won't work. I don't date men I work with."

Well, shit.

Kayla hated the smell of the Silver Valley Police Department's building. A small structure in the middle of the most commercial part of town, it seemed benign enough. Until she walked in and smelled the combination of day-old coffee, cigarette smoke and sugar. The coffee was self-explanatory. Any office that worked 24/7 needed a source of caffeine. The smoke wafted in from the outdoor designated smoking area, as all government buildings in Pennsylvania were smoke-free. The sugary scent she'd never been able to pinpoint. The likely stereotype was doughnuts, but the

SVPD employees she'd met, from the receptionist to police officers and detectives, were all in incredible physical shape.

Still, the smell of cotton-candy sugar lingered in the air.

She hated it because she associated the building with when her brother had been brought in to give a statement after the church fire last Christmas. She'd picked him up afterward.

The first time she'd had occasion to visit was also last Christmas, when her statement had to be taken and filed for her unintentional delivery of flowers from a serial killer.

This third time certainly wasn't the charm, she thought, as she sat in a cracked, padded chair in a drab interrogation room, waiting for someone to come take her statement—again.

She'd already told two different officers her version of events, from when she'd pulled up outside the barn until Rio had arrived on scene.

As if she was a suspect.

She felt like one, despite her guilt at not being able to do anything to save Meredith. Meredith, who'd been shot right in front of her, wasn't much younger than Kayla. She'd been doing her job as the mayor's assistant and in one horrible evening her life was over.

Kayla hadn't been able to do anything to save her own brother, Keith, from the evil that seemed to be invading Silver Valley, either. She'd been stunned when one of the couples from the church had filed a suit against Keith and the town, claiming they'd suffered from the fire and it was his fault. The mayor had said he sided with Keith but still removed him from active duty. He was still on administrative leave from the Silver Valley Fire Department.

Purposeful steps sounded on the other side of the door before Rio opened it and strode into the room. A smarter woman wouldn't have looked at him, but Kayla allowed herself a good long glance at the man she'd been unable to shake from her memory. She told herself it was the shock, not desire.

Rio.

It would be so much simpler if she hadn't slept with him. If she didn't know the passion beneath that rock-solid cop exterior. And he might be her only chance at proving she had nothing to do with this murder.

Rio was the one man she'd even considered starting a serious relationship with in years, until she realized how dangerous his occupation was. She'd dated a cop before, but with no intention of making it anything more than casual. Cops weren't available to her. Too risky. They could be killed. She'd had enough loss in her life. Being involved with someone she couldn't count on around-the-clock didn't appeal to her.

He lied to you.

He hadn't lied, really. Just left out one little fact about himself until it was too late for it to be an innocent oversight. If he didn't trust her with his real life from the get-go, she wanted no part of it.

"Here." He set a take-out latte in front of her. The sweet almond smell made her groan. He grinned.

"I thought you'd appreciate it about now. I'm sorry

you've had to wait for so long." He took the chair opposite her.

"Sure you are." She wasn't going to refuse the drink, however, and enjoyed several sips before she spoke again. "Thank you for the coffee. Let me guess, you need me to go over everything I've already told Officers Ogden and Miller?"

"No, you've given your official statement. I need you to dig a little deeper and think about your clientele. How many new customers have you had in the past few weeks?"

"You mean since the new mayor was installed?" She couldn't keep the sarcasm out of her tone. Rio's lips twitched. It would be so easy to reach over and make him smile.

Would have been, if they were still seeing each other. She really needed to get a grip. They'd barely dated. It had been more like a mutual lust-satisfaction gig. An arrangement Rio appeared to have forgotten.

"Since whenever. Anyone stick out, anyone seem strange, out of place in Silver Valley?"

She shook her head. "It's one of my busiest times of year, between Passover, Easter and springtime in general. Not as busy as Christmas, but it gets close to the same volume over the month. I can't always tell which new customers will stay and which ones are simply buying their bouquets for the season. But no one struck me as odd."

"What about your regular and special event contracts? You mentioned the current mayor is a regular customer?"

"The previous mayor is no longer on my regular list, of course, but yes, the new mayor picked up where she left off. Actually, his wife, Gloria, is the one who does the ordering." Ex-mayor Amelia Donner had started the tradition of keeping fresh flowers in the office while she was mayor and had extended it to her home. But these days Amelia Donner had no money for anything but her legal defense. "I do occasionally drop off some fresh flowers to Amelia."

"That's nice of you."

Kayla blushed. The latte warmed her fingers and she clung to the paper cup, wanting to drink more but not wanting to lose the source of comfort, afraid that her hands might still shake.

She risked a look at Rio, who remained his usual gorgeous self-contained "I am a detective, damn it" self. There was that flicker of light in his deep brown eyes, the flicker she missed. A lot.

He waited for her to think some more, remember something he could use. This was how Rio operated. As if he had all the time in the world. As if she was the only person he cared about.

"Gloria Charbonneau orders flowers fairly regularly for the same types of affairs as Mayor Donner did. But…" She took a large gulp of her drink.

"Go on."

"She isn't the friendliest person. She has very expensive taste and never wants the stems I have on hand. I have to go to the Port of Baltimore or Philadelphia for her requests and get the flowers fresh. I even had to go into New York once. I was surprised when she called about flowers for this wedding only because she's a careful planner, from my brief association with her. She doesn't do anything short-notice if she can help it."

"The wedding is a surprise from what you've said. And that corroborates the statements we've taken from the owner of the Weddings and More Barn."

"Yes, definitely short-notice. And I've never met her daughter, Cynthia. If she's anything like Gloria, the next week is going to be a rough one. Gloria is a per-fectionist, to say the least. You should be interviewing her, though, not me. I'm only the florist."

Rio's eyes lit up and his dimples, surprising in his masculine face, made Kayla smile.

"For being 'only the florist' you seem to get your-self in the middle of a lot of activity, Kayla."

"Spare me the official mumbo jumbo, Rio. You know me. You know it's all coincidence. It's a small town, and even if there are twenty thousand citizens of Silver Valley, there are only three other florists besides me, along with several more in the Harrisburg area. We each offer a different type of service." She shrugged, ready to be done. "You've taken my statements, and you know where I live. I'm not a flight risk. It's after midnight and my day starts in four hours with delivery preps for the local churches. May I go?"

He held her gaze long enough for her to see her emotions echoed in his expression. Feelings she had no desire to address, not at half-past midnight on a work night. On a night she'd witnessed a murder. On any night since they'd last been together as a couple.

"Yes, you can go. First let me make something very

clear. While I'm confident we'll clear you of any suspicious activities, that doesn't mean this is over. We have a murderer out there, someone who probably knew the victim. That means a local, and that means you could be on his radar. Your van was in full view. We're going to keep a close eye on you. Extra patrols past your shop at opening and closing, and by your home in the evenings. Don't be alarmed, we're just doing our job. But I would like you to stay quiet about what you saw last night. Don't volunteer to anyone that you were there—we told the owner of the Weddings and More Barn that it was a local who called in the report but we didn't say you were there. For all he knows, you drove up after the SVPD units arrived and went home."

"Sure, no problem." It wasn't something she wanted to discuss with anyone. "I'm telling you, the criminal never saw me or my van. Even if he made out the van down the drive, it was too dark and too far away to see the logo. I'm not concerned."

"It's not your decision whether or not we're concerned about your safety, Kayla. That's up to SVPD and we keep the people of Silver Valley safe."

"Tell that to Meredith Houseman."

His nostrils flared and in another place or situation she might have giggled. Instead immediate remorse made her angry at herself.

"I'm sorry, Rio. That was horrible of me to say. I know you would have done anything to save her." She knew that was true.

Rio said nothing as he yanked open the door.

"Officer Ogden, show Ms. Paruso out." His order

was sharp and she didn't expect him to say another word to her.

But he turned back to her and nodded.

"We're not done, Kayla. Expect to see more of me."

Chapter 5

Kayla opened the shop at five thirty the next morning. Sleep had been a losing proposition and after a few hours of tossing she got up and left for work.

The scent of hyacinths and Easter lilies permeated the air and she tried to allow the uplifting scents to raise her spirits. It didn't seem right to be putting together so many celebration arrangements while she still had the image of Meredith in her mind.

She sipped her coffee and winced at the bitter brew her stale beans had produced. She'd had no choice but to bring it from home as the local coffee shops weren't open for another thirty minutes. Her cupboards were bare; flower season left little time to get groceries. She could always run out later or have Jenny pick some up on the way in.

A solitary light over the workbench illuminated the long list of customers who required fresh flowers for their Passover and Easter celebrations, beginning with the Silver Valley Community Church. The historically significant edifice had almost burned to the ground at Christmas, with Zora and the man who was now her fiancé, Bryce, in the midst of the fire. Keith had been on scene with the SVFD and they'd gotten everyone out and had saved the historic building.

As Kayla snipped stems and stuck them into damp floral foam for a series of six matching arrangements, she allowed her mind to wander. Anywhere but to last night, which was still too scary to replay.

Of course Rio's dark brown eyes were the first image that appeared. Damn him. It would help to talk to someone about her feelings, but her sister, Melody, lived too far away, and Zora was in the midst of planning her wedding. Although even a bride-to-be needed a break, and Zora knew her best of anyone around.

Zora had been posing as a minister to help ferret out the serial killer who was after female preachers. Why Zora was involved in law enforcement, since she was a therapist, Kayla had never asked. Keith had told her not to, since it could compromise Zora if she was some kind of undercover agent. She'd been in the navy before, so Kayla wouldn't be surprised to find out Zora led two lives.

Together Zora and Bryce had brought down the serial killer who had used Kayla to take flowers, and a message, to Zora's college friend while she was acting as the congregation's interim pastor. Of course, it turned out that the "college friend" was really Zora, working undercover with SVPD.

Somehow during the case Zora had found love with Bryce, SVPD's other detective. Unlike Kayla, Zora seemed to have no issue with dating a cop.

A scraping noise alerted Kayla to the back door opening—the loading area for the van and incoming shipments. She fought back panic. It might not be an intruder, but she wasn't expecting Jenny for another two hours.

She grabbed for the largest pair of shears they kept at the workbench and held them in front of her with her right hand while her left reached for her phone.

"Kayla?" The familiar baritone washed away her anxiety with relief, followed by a quick, hot surge of anger.

"What are you doing here so early, Rio?"

He presented a paper bag and two cups of take-out coffee in a cardboard holder. "I knew you had an early start and wanted to make sure you're doing all right."

"You gave me coffee last night. That was enough."

"Still not a morning person, I see." He set the tray onto the counter and offered her one of the cups. "You can put the scissors down. You're safe. But I give you points for quick thinking."

She grudgingly lowered the makeshift weapon and accepted her second cup of coffee from Rio in less than twelve hours. Biting into the soft almond croissant she'd taken from the bag, she looked at him.

"These shears are no joke. They'd kill you as quick as a bullet if need be." He didn't react to her attempt at humor. She shifted her weight from foot to foot. "This is delicious, thank you. You couldn't have gotten much sleep, either." She remembered that he'd said he never slept much once he got into a case.

"I don't need a lot. You remember that, I'm sure."

The heat that had never disappeared between them suddenly scorched her insides and she wished she had more sense. That she had the wherewithal to tell him to get out of the shop and let the door hit him right on his sexy butt.

"Hmm."

"Hmm, indeed." His eyes took in everything. With a start she realized she missed this. The quiet morning time together, the intimacy of sharing the day's first cup of coffee as they woke up.

It was only three weeks. Get over it.

"I'm safe, Rio. As you can see, no one's here to bother me." Almost as if last night never happened.

"You're safe, my ass. I walked right in here. You didn't even have the back door locked!" His voice was quiet, low, but powered by the ferocity of his concern.

"I imagine it would be awful for you to lose your only witness."

"I'm not going to leave you high and dry, Kayla. You're not alone in this. We will catch this killer. And I know you're worried about Keith, and I assure you I'm working on that, too. Not every case takes as long as his has."

She didn't reply. She'd like to believe him that this case wouldn't languish as Keith's case continued to do.

Rio leaned against the bench and took a good long

perusal of the work area. "I don't think I ever got back here when we dated."

"No, you didn't." He'd come in the first time to order flowers for a colleague who was in the hospital. The next few times had been to pick her up after she closed shop and he'd waited in his car out front until she joined him. They hadn't wanted to spend time here—there was little room to do what they both wanted. What she had needed from him—his touch—was best experienced in a bedroom.

"You never answered my calls, Kayla."

So they were back to that.

"There was nothing to say. We'd agreed to stop seeing each other."

"And we'd agreed to stay friends. Friends keep in touch."

"Yeah, well, it's been busy."

Rio chugged his hot coffee as his mind replayed the hundreds of replies he could toss at Kayla in the morning quiet of the shop. They were both tired and on edge. She was probably still scared out of her wits, even though she'd never admit it to him.

But he saw it anyway, in the fine lines around her eyes, the slightly wild look she'd cast his way as he walked into the shop. If he hadn't called her name first, those ridiculously large scissors may have been lodged in his chest.

"It has. I'm glad for you, Kayla. I know how much the shop means to you." *Busy* meant that she'd increased her revenue and that the gossip about the serial killer ordering flowers from her hadn't tainted her business. It was hard to tell sometimes which way the whisper mill would turn in Silver Valley. Like the rumors around Kayla's brother's case. Rio still couldn't bring the case to closure, months after Keith Paruso had been accused of improper fire-inspection techniques and endangering public safety. Just when he thought he had Keith off the hook, another loophole was presented by the prosecuting attorney, in the shape of a couple Rio believed were being put up to do the dirty business of the cult. The former cult members had arrived just before all the political chaos began, but he had no definitive evidence they were connected to Keith's case. Yet.

"Thank you, and thanks for the coffee. It's a nice treat. With that in mind, I *do* need to keep working."

"Mind if I stay a bit and talk to you while you work?"

"Not at all."

He fought not to laugh. Her words were in direct opposition to the sour look on her face. He was the last person she wanted to spend time with.

"You know, Kayla, it seems a little silly to me that two people like us are allowing the past to control whether or not we have a cordial relationship until your brother's case is closed. We're intelligent adults." He watched her fingers move with equal parts grace and speed, stabbing pink flowers next to white in some kind of a green foam brick.

"Well, Rio—" God he loved how she said his name, and the images that refreshed for him "—I find it silly that you are standing here so early in the morning after a very long night in the police station, trying to pick up where we most definitely left off. I told you that it had nothing to do with you, personally. We agreed that we couldn't date, that it's a conflict of interest, remember? And I think being friends falls under that category, too."

"If I'd been a doctor and not told you what I did for that long, would you have been as upset?" She'd been angry that he hadn't been open about the fact that he worked undercover at times, and he'd been angry at himself for not putting it together that she was the fireman's sister.

Truth be told, he hadn't wanted to make the connection. All he'd wanted was to be with Kayla.

Two long spikes of green, maybe palm leaves, went into the middle of each of the arrangements. He wondered how she knew exactly where to place each stem so that the final product looked so perfect.

"Yes, I would have wondered why you hadn't told me what exactly you did."

"I told you I was a cop. And as soon as I was assigned directly to Keith's case, I should have asked to have it given to someone else."

"It doesn't matter now, does it?" She shook her head as she selected more blooms from a large plastic bin in the professional-grade refrigerator at the far back of the workroom. She shut the heavy door with her hip and the latch automatically clicked shut. "Stop watching my hips, Rio. It's distracting."

"Yes, ma'am. And for the record, it does matter.

Because we still obviously have some chemistry between us."

"Chemistry isn't enough to make something work when one partner is always gone. You disappeared in the middle of our, our…" She pursed her lips as she clipped away at unwanted leaves on the stems of some kind of purple flower.

"Our affair?"

He loved watching the color rise from her chest, bared by her crewneck, up her neck and across her cheekbones. It reminded him of the other ways, one in particular, that he'd made her blush so profusely.

"Whatever you want to call it."

He laughed. "Kayla, you are hands-down the most complicated woman I've ever known."

"Thank you, I think?" She put her gloved fists on her hips. "Rio, I understand that you're here because you've probably been assigned to keep an eye on me. You and I know I'm nothing more than a witness—I wasn't involved in the murder. Do what you need to do to get your job done. But don't think you have to sugarcoat it with fancy coffee and polite conversation. We're not supposed to be talking to each other, remember?"

"We can't discuss your brother's case, that's all. And I'm not a sugarcoating kind of guy, Kayla. You know that. I'm here because I want to be. You can have SVPD cops checking in on you, but the regular presence of uniformed police in your shop probably isn't the best thing for business, is it?"

"My customers aren't afraid of the police, if that's what you're asking. Your colleagues crawled all over my shop at Christmas, after I delivered the flowers to Zora from the Female Preacher Killer. It didn't hurt business then."

He had to level with her.

"We're watching the new mayor closely." He watched *her* as he explained. "You mentioned that his wife frequents your shop. And now, with the wedding this weekend, it's a good opportunity to try to learn more about them."

"You're using my business as your cover?"

"Not exactly. We need you to help us out."

"I already told you, I'll keep my eyes and ears open."

"That's good, Kayla, but I need you to be careful. If the mayor is who we think he is, associated with the kinds of people we suspect, he's a dangerous man."

"Which is why his assistant is dead, I presume?"

"Maybe." He hesitated, knowing he shouldn't share everything with her, but somehow needing to. "Kayla, I suspect that whoever is behind your brother's civil suit may be tied to the mayor, as well. I can't say much more, but trust me when I tell you there's a chance that as we delve into this murder investigation we may uncover some ugly facts."

"Any chance the facts could clear Keith?"

"Yes, that's what I'm hoping for, but again, I can't promise you anything. You know that if Keith's case goes to trial I'll be stating that I don't believe the charges against him are valid. And I shouldn't say any more." She looked so damn hopeful and he hated putting the encouragement out there when he, more than anyone, knew it could end up being a long haul. "I can't say anything else about Keith, Kayla. And trust me when I tell you that the people on the other end of this, the persons I suspect the mayor may have ties to, are wily and loaded. It's an uphill battle. Their coffers run deep and money keeps otherwise nonsensical claims alive in court."

She snorted as she clipped the stems of several daisy-type flowers.

He watched as her tongue darted out to moisten her lower lip. "Kayla?"

"You think Keith's innocent, too. Don't you?"

He looked at her. Knew he shouldn't do what he was going to do, what he'd wanted to do since he'd walked into her shop. Since he saw her last night, shivering in shock at the barn. Since he'd last made love to her, four months ago.

Her eyes were tired; she'd been up most of the night, as had he. But they reflected the same spark of attraction that he felt, the combustible chemistry that was making him hard. He reached out and cupped her jaw. "You're beautiful, Kayla." He didn't have to pull her to him—she leaned in for the kiss.

When their lips met there was no pretense of it being a first kiss again, or a simple affectionate gesture. Her mouth pressed against his with equal force and when he slid his tongue between her lips she met it with hers. Rio stopped thinking and let Kayla's moist breath, her soft gasps, her urgent caresses against his upper arms, take him away from the gravity of the case.

Her arms went up around his neck and he took the opportunity to cup her breasts as they kissed, then moved his hands to her firm butt and gently pressed her against his erection. Her work counter was up against his back and he used the support to take most of her weight, forcing her onto her tiptoes.

"I want you, Kayla. I've never stopped wanting you."

Her reply was a quick nip to his lower lip before he felt cool air against his face. He reluctantly opened his eyes and found her stare unnerving.

"We aren't supposed to be doing this, Rio."

"I know." He stroked the distinctly feminine curve of her lower back and watched as she bit her lower lip, trying to hold back the moan he wanted to hear.

"Stop, Rio."

He lowered his arms and she took a step back. Her face was as bright pink as the tulips on the worktable and he couldn't miss her hard nipples as they pushed against her shirt.

"I'm sorry, Kayla. When I'm around you my dick does the thinking."

"That's all it is, Rio?" Her tone cooled as quickly as he'd heated up during their kiss.

"We never lasted long enough to find out if it could be more."

"Your career is your first priority." She sniffed and picked up a bunch of green stems with fluffy leaves.

"And you don't want to date a cop. And you can't trust me, right? We're back to square one."

"Not exactly." Challenge lit her expression. "We both want my brother's name cleared. And I want to see this mayor get his due if he's a bad guy. So do you. Let me help out as much as I can with the Charbonneaus."

"No heroic measures, Kayla."

"Fine, but if I get a chance to dig up dirt, I won't stop." They both grinned at her unintended pun.

Rio held out his hand. "Friends? For now?"

She grasped his hand and shook, nodding. "For now. I'm willing to do whatever it takes to get these bastards, whoever they are. My brother is a gifted firefighter and law-enforcement officer. He needs to be doing his job."

"Trust me, Silver Valley needs him to be doing his job." He let her hand go only when he had to. Otherwise he would have tugged her back for another kiss.

Chapter 6

"You've done a lot this morning." Jenny stared at the dozens of arrangements placed strategically across every spare inch of floor, counter and shelf space in the workroom. Kayla followed her gaze, realizing she hadn't stopped since Rio had left over an hour ago.

"I couldn't sleep. I—" She stopped herself. She couldn't mention last night. "I, um, guess it's catching up to me."

"Want me to start putting them in the van?"

"Yes, thanks. The list is over there." She motioned to the bulletin board, where she had each day's deliveries tacked in neat piles.

"Got it." Jenny lifted two of the smaller arrangements and went out the back door. Kayla watched her and used the time to stretch. And tried to ignore the warmth that still lingered from Rio's visit. Rio was like that—he filled whatever space he entered with positive energy. She'd never gotten much out of him about where he was from, or his childhood, but she assumed he came from a loving family since he had so much warmth under his cool cop exterior.

The silent vibration on her phone alerted her to the shop's opening time. She made her way to the front of the building, flipping on the lights as she went. The bright blooms inside the shop's refrigerated display case brought a bit of a smile to her face, even the morning after she'd witnessed a brutal murder.

Before she had the sound system turned on, the bell over the door announced a customer.

Gloria Charbonneau. The attractive woman sauntered into the shop as if it was her domain and not Kayla's.

"Good morning, Kayla. How are you today?"

"Good morning to you, too, Gloria." She forced a smile and didn't dare call Gloria "Mrs. Charbonneau," as she'd been rebuffed by Gloria when she'd addressed her as such over the phone.

"I thought we'd better do an in-person chat rather than another phone conversation. I am so sorry about my call yesterday. I sounded so frantic, didn't I? But when Cynthia announced she was getting married and threatened to elope to Las Vegas—" Gloria said the words *elope* and *Las Vegas* as if they were coated with venom "—I had to make sure that didn't happen. I mean, if she's going to elope she should pay homage to her roots and go to Atlantic City, right?" Gloria chortled at her own joke. "No matter now. I've calmed her down, and she decided to give us almost two full weeks to plan a nice affair for her."

Kayla wanted to point out that it was already Wednesday, and they actually had only a business week to plan.

"Next weekend is much easier than this weekend would have been, with Passover and Easter at the same time this year."

"I thought so. Who wants to compete with the Easter Bunny, after all?" Gloria's face was perfectly composed as she flitted about the shop, made up with what Kayla suspected was a cosmetics chest full of ultra-expensive lotions, creams and serums. Gloria couldn't be much older than Kayla but acted as if she was of her husband's generation. Tony Charbonneau was at least twenty years her senior. As polished as Gloria appeared, Kayla saw the nervous tic over Gloria's right eye and how tight her hand held her car keys while a wristlet dangled from her arm. No amount of makeup could hide her tension.

Was she here to find out if Kayla had gone to the barn last night?

"Your home decor items are precious!" She held up a frog statuette. The green tchotchke contrasted with Gloria's black clothing. She was decked out in the finest yoga gear and her figure screamed the hours she must spend in the gym. Kayla and she were the same age, but Gloria could pass for much younger.

Save for her overbearing, overcontrolling manner. That usually took decades to cultivate.

"I was wondering, did you have a chance to go by the barn last night?" Innocent enough, if not for the tic that continued to twitch over her eye.

Kayla swallowed. "No, I'm afraid I couldn't swing it. I plan to go today." Thank God Rio had told her how to handle this in advance.

"Great! I mean, I'd hate to have you waste your time. We've decided to have the wedding ceremony at our home. We're getting a minister now, and the vows will be said in our garden. I'm having a tent put in next to the gazebo in case of inclement weather. We'll have the reception at the same venue as the rehearsal dinner."

Kayla surreptitiously bit the inside of her lower lip, a nervous habit she meant to break. *Holy crap!* Maybe Gloria *was* involved in the murder. At the very least she knew *something*. She'd changed the venue that she'd sounded so definite about last night. Before Meredith had been killed.

Kayla's cell phone rang and she tried to appear casual as she looked at the caller ID. Rob Owings, owner of the Weddings and More Barn. She sent Gloria a quick glance.

"I'm so sorry, Gloria, but I have to take this. Why don't you take a look at my wedding-idea file while I do?"

"Of course." Gloria accepted the tablet computer from Kayla without protest.

"Tap on whichever suits your fancy, and we'll come up with something together. I'll be right back."

Kayla moved to the far rear of the shop, where she could keep an eye on Gloria but still have some privacy.

"Kayla here."

"Kayla, it's Rob."

"I know."

"Oh, you have a customer. Look, I'm not sure if you know what happened at the barn last night—did you ever make it out there?"

"I drove by and saw the police cars. I found out someone had died from one of the SVPD and decided to go home. I didn't call you because I knew the police would have to be in touch with you. I didn't want to interfere." Lying was easier than people claimed, she decided. Still, it stung that she couldn't be open with Rob.

"I'm so glad you weren't there, Kayla. Someone was murdered." Static on the line indicated he was probably moving about as he spoke. "I know I'm being selfish but it'd kill my business if the news got out. It's going to hit the papers soon enough, but I don't need the town gossip mill going over it before that even happens." Rob's shaky inhalation wasn't like him. "Anyway, I wanted to give you a heads-up that the mayor's wife's assistant just called and canceled the venue. She didn't seem to know anything about last night, only said that they'd decided to move the ceremony to their home. I'm sure she'll be in touch with you soon."

"Thanks for letting me know, Rob." She couldn't say anything more.

"I'm sure we'll get to work together again soon, Kayla. Without all of this craziness."

"I'm sure we will, too."

"Just answer me this, Kayla—you got there after

that woman was killed, right? Or did you see something?"

Chills ran down her spine and across her forearms. Rob's prying wasn't unusual for him; he was a friendly guy. But after Rio's warnings, she felt ambushed.

"No, as I said, I saw the cops and after I talked to a friend from SVPD, someone I recognized, I went home." Her exhaustion was paying off in that her voice didn't waver.

Rob breathed an audible sigh. "I'm sure glad of that. You could have been hurt—you never know about people, do you?"

"No, no, you don't. Thanks for letting me know, Rob," she said again. "I have to go, I have a customer standing in front of me."

"Understand. I'll be in touch."

Kayla stared at Gloria as the woman's perfectly manicured fingers tapped through wedding photos, but her mind was on Rob. His shape was a little round, his voice was low and gravelly—like the murderer's, from what she'd heard and seen in the darkness. But it hadn't been Rob—Rob didn't have a mean bone in his body.

"Do you see anything you like?"

Gloria smiled, her expression so practiced that Kayla wondered if she did mirror exercises.

"These are all very sweet, but I have my own ideas. Can you come with me to the house?"

"Sure. Let's set up an appointment. You said you want to have the wedding next week, on Saturday?"

"Yes. Thank goodness I calmed Cynthia down and she agreed to give me one more week to plan."

"Why don't we set up a time when she can be there, too?"

Gloria's eyes widened. "That's a little difficult. She's in her last semester of law school and is taking a weekend to get married before her exams. It's a lot to ask her to drive back and forth for the planning."

"She must be very smart to be able to take the time from her studies to get married before she finishes."

Gloria shrugged. "The bar exam is the hard test, I'm told. Not the law school finals."

Kayla didn't argue, but personally thought getting married during any kind of final exam would be difficult at best.

"When can I stop by?"

"In two hours? I'll provide lunch."

"Thank you. I'll be there."

"Hi, Daddy."

"Hi, sweetheart. How's my girl?" Mayor Tony Charbonneau stood to greet his daughter. Cynthia was a full head shorter than her father, but her face was a feminine mirror of his, albeit far more attractive.

Rio watched the affectionate display with the detachment that years of police work had given him. Nothing was ever as good as it seemed. Rio's own father had been killed in Mexico, working as a DEA agent to take down a dangerous drug cartel. Rio wanted to believe every father was as honest and self-sacrificing as his own, but he knew from his work that was not the case.

Especially with Tony Charbonneau, who oozed slick politician the way a Bengal tiger stalking its prey oozed predator.

"Who are you?" Cynthia spotted Rio only after she'd stepped back from her father's embrace.

"Detective Rio Ortega, Silver Valley PD." He watched her open expression with the ferocity of a cornered badger. He gave her points for maintaining her composure, however, as she held her hand out to him.

"Cynthia Charbonneau." He took her hand and noted that her grip was firm and practiced. As if she knew how to shake a man's hand. Not all women did. "I suppose you're here because of what happened to poor Meredith?" She looked from Rio to her father, her concern...proper. As expected.

"Yes, Detective Ortega was just finishing up, weren't you?"

"Actually, no. If you don't mind I'd like to continue to ask you a few more questions, and also ask Cynthia some if that's okay, Mayor."

Tony Charbonneau's throat turned red and the flush crept up his heavy jowls, but he kept his smile pleasant, his demeanor casual. "Of course." He motioned to the chairs in front of his desk. "Why don't you sit down for a bit, Detective?"

Rio didn't miss the gibe. He'd refused to sit earlier, preferring to stay on his feet around the man who'd gotten into office only because of what Rio believed was a political attack on the former mayor that had removed her from office posthaste. The special election had worked in Mayor Charbonneau's favor, too. Many people had questioned the election results, but after an intense investigation there'd been no evidence of wrongdoing with the election, so no charges had been filed. The only charges filed were against the former mayor, Amelia Donner, who was looking at three to five years in a white-collar holding facility if she lost her case. The case against her was being championed by an attorney directly tied to the former cult. Rio hoped the pressure SVPD was putting on the former cult members would reveal a way to clear Mayor Donner's name.

"Cynthia, when did you come back in from law school?"

"Yesterday, before noon. It's only a twenty minute drive from Carlisle. I'm in the Penn State law program at Dickinson College. I have an apartment there."

"Do you have friends who were with you at school before you left?"

"Yes. We were studying for our finals in the library for the past few weeks, and we've started to prepare our study schedules for the bar. We'll only have three months to study after graduation."

"And you have contacts I may question about this?"

"Of course, but is that really necessary?"

"I'm conducting a murder investigation. Every question is necessary. Mayor, when did you see Cynthia last?"

Tony's head drew back and his brows rose. "What, do you mean when she got home? I guess it was after work, wasn't it, honey?"

"Yes, but you were late because you were answering police questions."

"Yes, that's right."

"Cynthia, who was the first person to see you when you got back into town?"

"My stepmother, Gloria. She was in the shower when I came in, early yesterday morning. I stayed downstairs and made a pot of coffee, which we shared when she came downstairs a while later."

"Did the housekeeper or your mother's personal assistant see you?"

"Once they arrived for work, yes, but I got in very early."

"I guess that's student life—burning the candle at both ends. So you studied until late and then drove to Silver Valley early. You got up at what, four o'clock?"

"I've always been an early riser, Detective Ortega." She'd sure been through law school. Quick on her feet, sure of herself. He didn't begrudge her that but her alibi wasn't sitting well with him. He revealed nothing to either her or her father.

"And, Mayor, approximately what time did you see Cynthia? Please be as specific as possible."

"It would have had to been around six thirty or so, when I came home. Gloria was out at her spinning class at the gym. We ordered pizza and started in on a six-pack of Yuengling." The mayor grinned. "We love to drink locally brewed beer wherever we live, and it's our favorite. Our father-daughter thing."

If Rio wasn't a detective he'd be taken in by the happy-family shtick. He wouldn't see the two very sim-

ilar political animals in front of him. Tony was a hard-
ened politician who'd been drummed out of New Jersey
for his nefarious dealings in local politics, a point that
had come up during the mayoral race two months ago.
But accounts of his history hadn't gained traction if his
landslide victory was to be believed. Rio didn't doubt
for one instant that the election results had been tam-
pered with, but he wasn't an expert in such matters.
He was looking for a murderer.

"Mayor, I need you to stay in town for the next few
weeks. Cynthia, I'll need to be able to contact you at
any time. I know you have to go back to school before
the wedding, and that's fine, since you're close enough
in Carlisle."

"You think you'll have the murderer by then?" he
asked.

"I have law school to finish! I can't be disturbed
when I'm studying."

Both Charbonneaus spoke in rapid-fire sentences
and Rio held up his hands. "Sorry, folks, it's standard
procedure during a murder investigation."

"We're not suspects. How can you ask us to stay?"

"You are both persons of interest. You, Mayor, because Meredith worked for you and you were the last
person to see her alive, right here in this office." He
pointed at Cynthia. "Your timing for coming home
from law school is questionable. You understand, it's
just protocol."

Tony recovered a beat sooner than his daughter.

"We're here to give you whatever you need, Detective. Meredith was a good worker, even if she had some personal problems."

"What kind of problems?"

"She was a little obsessive. Her record keeping, for instance—she kept asking me to purchase more computer servers for storage space. The last time I saw her I had to tell her to stop worrying about making copies of everything and just do her job as my assistant."

"My dad means that he thought she might have some OCD," Cynthia said, and Rio thought it was a good effort at trying to cover for her father's slip. One thing Rio knew about criminals was that they often overcompensated for their guilt. Tony had no reason to tell him about Meredith's mental issue unless he was trying to deflect Rio's attention.

"OCD?"

"Obsessive-compulsive disorder. It makes sense as she was so incredibly organized. I wish I had a little of that myself." Cynthia's quick laugh was hollow and completely inappropriate, Rio thought.

"Are you saying that Meredith's mental state might have brought about her murder?"

"No, not at all."

"Of course not!"

Again, father and daughter spoke over one another.

"That's good to hear, because for a minute it sounded to me as if you were discounting the brutal, vicious way Meredith was murdered."

He felt the anger of two intelligent people boring into him. Nothing he hadn't experienced before, but what he hadn't felt in quite a while, not since he'd taken down a drug ring three years ago, was the sense of pure hatred he felt from the mayor and his daughter. As if Rio was the enemy.

Interesting.

Chapter 7

Kayla was happy to be able to drive with the windows down. The unseasonably warm air swept through the van's front seat. She'd texted Rio to let him know she was going to her appointment with Gloria, since she'd promised to keep him informed of her contact with the Charbonneaus.

What she wasn't going to tell him was that she was planning to do some investigating of her own. When Keith was charged with negligence, she'd learned to hold her suspicious thoughts and hunches close while she acted on them. And it was always easier to ask for forgiveness than permission.

Keith had found his calling as a firefighter and risen to the top of his game when he'd been promoted to chief years ahead of his contemporaries. He'd helped get an aging firefighting squad in shape and provided Silver Valley with one of the best teams in the state. That was why the blow dealt to his career last Christmas still had him, and all of SVFD, reeling. He'd been blamed for the fire that had been started by a psychopathic killer, all because his crew hadn't found the accelerant before the Christmas service. Kayla was shocked when he told her he was being investigated for other crimes he hadn't committed, including not getting the churchgoers out of the burning building fast enough.

Someone wanted Keith out of SVFD. The more she thought about it, the more she suspected that maybe the same person or persons wanted to dismantle SVFD entirely. Not unlike what had happened to Mayor Donner. It certainly seemed that someone was trying to tear apart the solid community Silver Valley had been only six months ago.

As she pulled to a stop at a light in the center of downtown Silver Valley, she took a moment to take in the budding trees. The forsythia had already burst forth and the lilac trees were almost in full bloom. Silver Valley had such a small-town feel, but the population of over twenty thousand afforded it all the conveniences of a sprawling suburban community. Without the traffic and, usually, without the kind of crime she'd stumbled upon last night.

Kayla turned the van onto a stately street lined with houses that dated back three centuries. The Charbonneaus lived in a well-preserved Victorian home. The outside was painted hunter green and the gingerbread trim was creamy yellow with gilt highlights. She wondered if Gloria would prefer living in one of the many upscale developments in the more suburban parts of Silver Valley, with their McMansion-style decor. Something closer to her and the mayor's showy taste.

The mayor of Silver Valley needed to reside in the historical town proper, however, so the Charbonneaus had purchased the Victorian a month before he was elected to office. A bold move considering the election had been expected to go to a younger politician who was well-known in town for her athletic accomplishments, first at Silver Valley High and then at Georgetown University in Washington. Now retired from women's basketball and returned to her hometown, Poppy Hopper had been a shoe-in.

Until Anthony Charbonneau showed up.

Parallel parking in between two Priuses wasn't easy, but Kayla did it, since there were no driveways in Silver Valley's historical district. The fuel-efficient cars were as ubiquitous as the Bradford pear trees that dominated much of the local landscape.

The home's front porch was wide and welcoming, and a hand-painted sign declared Mayor and Gloria Charbonneau resided there. Kayla rolled her eyes at a tiny chipmunk that was busy studying her from one of the potted tulips she'd delivered last week. He twitched his whiskers and darted out of sight. It reminded her that she needed to tend to the flower beds in her own garden, but it would have to wait. With everything she had scheduled, the chipmunks would probably eat all her bulbs by the time she had a chance to put her fingers in the soil again.

The door opened as Kayla lifted her hand. Only then did she notice the unobtrusive security camera set in the middle of the door knocker.

"You must be Kayla. Gloria is in the dining room. Let me show you back."

"Thank you." Kayla smiled. "And you are?"

"I'm Sylvia, Gloria's personal assistant."

"Nice to meet you in person." They'd spoken on the phone when Sylvia placed the orders for official functions, as well as for the house. Jenny handled most of the weekday deliveries.

Kayla noted that Gloria's weekly arrangement sat on a pedestal table on the right side of the hallway, where every visitor would see the fresh flowers. She hoped many asked Gloria where she'd purchased them.

"Kayla, please, have a seat." Gloria sat on one side of the huge maple wood table, motioning for Kayla to take the seat opposite. The table appeared to be set for formal tea, with the china clearly matching the period of the house.

"This is beautiful." Kayla felt a little out of place in her usual work outfit—black leggings and a V-neck purple pullover with her shop logo embroidered over the left breast. At least she'd taken the time to run her fingers through her pixie cut.

"Yes, we've taken measures to keep everything as authentic as possible. It's so important to preserve Silver Valley's history."

Kayla smiled in an attempt to appear sociable. While she adored flowers and natural beauty, Kayla was more interested in a person's character than outward appearances. Gloria's passion appeared to be outward appearances, not unusual for a politician's wife.

"Please, dig in and enjoy your meal while I outline my plans for Cynthia's ceremony."

Kayla took a generous swig of the iced tea from a crystal glass and settled into her meal as best she could while Gloria went through list after list of the flowers she'd need for each room of the house. Her note cards were embossed with her name in gold ink and she used a fountain pen that probably cost more than Kayla's Blooms made in six months.

"We'll need everything fresh, crisp and with no signs of wilting anywhere."

"Of course. That's what I do." Kayla smoothed the pale blush napkin on her lap. "I'll make up all the arrangements as close to the ceremony as possible. We will need to get the gazebo done the evening before."

"But what if we have a very hot night? Or if we get a late freeze?" Gloria's Botoxed forehead allowed just enough expression for Kayla to make out her genuine concern.

"I'll worry about that. If it was still this coming Saturday, we'd have more to worry about, but the weather report looks okay temperature-wise. They used to say we'd be free of frost worries any time after Mother's Day, but the past ten years have been milder."

Mother's Day was the hallmark date used by gardeners in the central Pennsylvania region to mark the full arrival of spring.

"We had an awful winter and I read that the ground is having a hard time warming up. Don't you think we should wait until the morning of to put out the garden arrangements?" Unlike anyone else in Silver Valley, Gloria used the European term *garden* for backyard. Kayla had to keep from smiling.

"Let's not worry about that today. I'll do whatever needs to be done to make the day perfect for you." Thank God she only had to worry about flowers and not the cake or wedding dress.

"Oh, and I'd like you to coordinate with the baker so that the cake has similar flowers."

"No problem."

"I'm using the best bakery in Harrisburg. You'll need to go out there, since Veronique is too busy to come to Silver Valley."

Kayla was grateful for the tuna salad in her mouth so that she didn't have to bite her lip until she sprayed blood on Gloria's fine linens. She'd had to work with Veronique Bleu twice before and both times had been a challenge. Veronique had grown up in the Harrisburg area as Veronica Bluestone, but after graduating from the Le Cordon Bleu she came back to the area a born-again Francophile. Her baked goods were phenomenal and until Kayla had met the difficult woman behind the concoctions she'd treated herself to one of the bakery's éclairs on special occasions.

"I know Veronique. We've worked together before."

"Really? She didn't mention it, but then, she is very busy. Her cakes are sent all over the world."

Yes, Kayla knew this, too. No matter. It was her job to work with the baker and so she would.

Gloria's assistant appeared in the dining room.

"Gloria, you have a call in your office."

Gloria looked at her assistant and Kayla watched an emotion she never associated with her play across her face. Fear.

"Please excuse me. I'll have the tea and dessert brought out."

Kayla nodded, wondering where she'd put any more food after the rich lunch. As soon as Sylvia and Gloria were out of sight, Kayla quietly pushed back from the table and went out in to the hallway. Voices drifted through two closed antique doors as old as the house.

"I told you to tell him I'm in a meeting."

"I'm sorry but he insisted he had to speak to you."

"Stay here. I want a witness."

A witness?

"Hello, Tony."

"Gloria. You didn't put me on speakerphone, did you?" She recognized the mayor's voice as Gloria must have indeed put the call on speakerphone.

"I did, but only because I'm in the middle of sorting files. Don't worry, I'm alone in my office. Sylvia is keeping the florist busy in the dining room. How are you, darling?"

Why was she lying to her husband?

"Up to my ass in alligators. It's a pain in the neck, this job. We should have kept our focus on the big race and not taken this detour. And now we have to find me a new assistant. Have you gotten anywhere on that this morning?"

"I'm working on it."

"Remember what I said. Don't let Cynthia's wedding planning take precedence over this, Gloria. We need a new assistant and I can't be the one looking for her. It wouldn't be smart, not this soon."

"The wedding will take care of itself, darling. Cynthia is a simple girl who doesn't want a big fuss. For your assistant, I was thinking of a man this time, Tony."

If this was a "simple" wedding Kayla did not want to know what kind of wedding Gloria considered lavish. There was a long pause and Kayla wondered if Gloria had turned off the speaker.

"Whatever, Gloria. I need someone eager enough to be willing to do what we need without being too nosy or concerned about all my personal projects."

What kind of projects?

"I know that, Tony. I'm only looking out for you, sweetheart."

"You always do. And thanks for the bag of burner phones. You're always a step ahead of me."

"I didn't expect we'd need them this soon, but I'm glad you have them."

"Yeah, I'm sure the cops will be looking at me since Meredith was out there on my dime, but there's no connection."

"No, honey, of course there's not. But you don't need the added stress of an investigation right now."

"The florist, did you get a chance to talk to her?"

"I did one better. She's going to work with us on Cynthia's wedding here."

"Is that a good idea? Maybe you should hire someone else."

"She never got out there last night. Doesn't know a thing about it."

"How can you be sure?"

"I know how to keep my enemies close, Tony."

Kayla felt a single drop of perspiration make its way from the nape of her neck to the small of her back as she stood stock-still on the hall carpet. Just how close *did she* want to be to these people?

Maybe Rio was right. She was a florist, not a detective.

"Excuse me, who are you?" Kayla jumped at the voice behind her. She stepped back from Gloria's office door as if she'd been burned. She faced a young woman with a no-nonsense brunette bob and the palest blue eyes she'd ever seen.

"I'm Kayla. I'm Ms. Charbonneau's florist."

"What are you doing standing here?" This had to be Cynthia. Her resemblance to her father was unmistakable.

"I needed to let Ms. Charbonneau know I'm leaving, but I didn't want to interrupt anything important. And you're…?" No way was a Charbonneau going to get the better of her. She reminded herself to stay cool. This job was too important to lose.

"I'm Cynthia." Just like her father, a bright, wide smile and slight head tilt transformed Cynthia into a personable being, someone Kayla could easily see in front of a jury or an audience of voters. "It's my wedding that you're planning."

"Oh, I'm so pleased to meet you. Your mother said you were finishing up final exams for law school."

A slight narrowing of her eyes was Cynthia's only sign that she might not like it that Gloria had been talking about her. "Stepmother. Gloria's my *step*mother. My *real* mother split when I was a baby. And I'm almost finished with my exams, which is why I could come home for a quick visit today, before I have to study for my final presentation—they're a big deal, you know—and then start studying for the bar exam in July. I'm literally up the road at Dickinson College. The Penn State law program." She laughed. "Mostly, though, I just couldn't wait to marry Charles, even if the timing is a bit crazy."

"Charles is your fiancé, I assume?" Kayla hadn't thought to ask the groom's name yet. And how was Cynthia able to talk so readily about her mother abandoning her?

"Yes, Charles Blackwell, the judge. Perhaps you've heard of him?" Cynthia smiled sweetly but Kayla detected the sense of victory underneath her query. As if her future husband was her trophy. Kayla swallowed her laughter. The parallel of the mayor and his daughter having trophy spouses didn't escape her.

"Yes, he's in the paper a lot."

"Yes, he is. He's met the president." Cynthia smacked her lips as if she'd taken a mouthful of the world's most expensive caviar. "I am so excited for us to be married. We share a common passion for politics and government."

"Lovely." Kayla smiled and prayed she looked mesmerized instead of completely baffled. It was as if she'd been dropped into a bizarre television drama.

"Lovely?"

"I mean, being so in love. A last-minute wedding is so romantic."

"It's not that last-minute. Our marriage has been in the planning stages for at least a month now. The wedding is just a day. Isn't that what they say?" Cynthia raised an eyebrow as if she dared Kayla to contradict her. Kayla wasn't a big believer in things "they" said, whoever "they" were.

"The wedding day is important, too, though—it can set the tone for a marriage. It's definitely worth it to start your life together with a special day." How many brides had she uttered these words to, believing them but never believing it would happen in her life? Kayla wasn't so keen on marriage. Why did Rio pop into her head as she thought that? Marriage would be especially difficult with someone who had a job as crazy as his. Kayla could see herself living with someone maybe. A commitment for life, however, would mean risking the stability she had carved out for herself. Stability wasn't something she was willing to give up.

Loneliness would be a good thing to give up.

"Our day will be wonderful, of course. Charles has told me to do whatever I want." Cynthia leaned in closely to Kayla, as if they were longtime confidantes. "He's been married twice before. It's not common knowledge, but he's had a run of bad luck with wives. He was divorced early from his first wife and was married to his second wife for over twenty years. He was widowed last year."

"Oh?" Kayla didn't want to know such personal details but if it gave her insight into this crazy family and a lead on who killed Meredith, she was all ears.

"Yes. Both of his exes had drinking problems. A lack of self-control can have terrible consequences. I'm just happy Charles won't have to worry about that with me."

Kayla bit the inside of her cheek to keep from uttering her opinion that addiction wasn't a choice. Let Cynthia have it however she wanted it—Kayla was here to supply the flowers and help the SVPD solve a crime. It was the only leverage she might have to help Rio get the killer and free up his time to work on Keith's case.

"Well, I need to let your stepmother know I've done my preliminary walk-through and I'll be back to take more detailed measurements. She had her office door closed—I didn't want to interrupt her."

Cynthia stared at her a beat too long, during which Kayla wiggled her toes in her shoes. "No problem. I'll let her know you've finished. I'm sure we'll be seeing a lot of you over the next ten days. It's going to be a wonderful wedding."

"Absolutely, it will."

Kayla let herself out the front door and fought the impulse to shake her head in disbelief. The vast majority of brides she'd worked with were so happy and nervous about their nuptials that they talked about nothing else. Cynthia wasn't exactly a typical bride-to-be.

What kind of bride will you be?

No kind. After being burned by her time with Rio, and still having to fight her attraction to him almost half a year later, long-term anything wasn't on Kayla's agenda. Not until her heart healed, as much as she hated to admit it even to herself. And even then, the man she eventually picked for a lifetime had to want to be in a safer position. Not fighting bad guys and risking his life every day.

Not that she was thinking about weddings and Rio together.

She'd leave the weddings to her clients.

Chapter 8

"Hi, Kayla." Keith, her tall, sandy-haired brother, opened the front door to his townhome and accepted the bag of groceries she'd brought. "I'm not starving, you know. I'm still getting paid." He closed the door behind them and followed her into the kitchen.

"I cooked some extra soup, some casseroles and lasagna last weekend. They're frozen but all you have to do is thaw and heat them up and you'll have a quick meal. I figured you're so busy with your case that you'd be able to use some meals you don't have to cook yourself." Her brother hated the idea of her feeling sorry for him.

"We're adults, sis. The older-sibling mantle is wearing thin on your shoulders."

That was just like Keith, making her smile when he was in such grim circumstances.

"Let me be the big sis while I can. Someday you might be taking care of me in a nursing home."

"Doubtful. You're the most active person I know, besides the guys at the station. Between your business and yoga class, not to mention cooking pity meals for me, you never stop." He eased onto his sofa, only a few feet from the kitchen counter in his small living space. "Have you heard from Mom and Dad?" Kayla knew what he was really asking was *Do they still think I'm innocent?*

"They'll be back in town in two weeks or so. They asked if one of us could freshen up their place and put some basics in the refrigerator." Her dad was long retired from diplomatic service, but her mother had her own international decor store in town. They were on the road through Poland and Russia at the moment, ordering pottery and wooden Santa dolls for the start of the Christmas season in six months. Their shop had to be prepared in September to appease the appetites of their voracious collectors, who preferred to shop early for the winter holidays. Silver Valley had been the home of both sets of Kayla's grandparents and a natural place to retire once both Kayla and Keith started attending Penn State. Their older sister, Melody, had gone to Oberlin College and worked for the State Department. She lived in Africa with her husband.

"When will they get in?"

"They're flying into Harrisburg early on the weekend after Easter."

"It's the longest they've been gone to order stock."

"I think they miss the old life. I won't be surprised if they add a visit to see Melody."

He nodded. "Nothing like how we grew up, moving around as if we were jet-setters."

She laughed and he joined her. Their life had been far from materially rich as they'd traveled from embassy to embassy with the smallest collection of belongings. The furniture had always been provided, as had the appliances and basic cookware. The rest had been improvised according to the customs of the country they lived in.

"Those experiences were priceless, though. And you know they miss us, too. They're not getting any younger."

"Neither is my case," he grumbled. Keith wasn't self-pitying, but the case was wearing on him. "This is beyond inane. My record speaks for itself."

"So why aren't you being acquitted more readily?" She sat in the easy chair opposite him.

"Someone has a hard-on for the SVFD. They want us shut down, period."

"That's ridiculous. We need a fire department!"

"There's a faction of the community who think the firefighting duties should entirely belong to the counties, not the municipalities. It's about cash flow and taxation. And then the volunteer issue…"

"What do *you* think, Keith?"

His eyes flashed angrily before he blinked and let out a long sigh.

"I don't know what's better economically and

frankly I don't care about that side of it. What I know is that you have to have local firefighters who know the area like the back of their hand in order to keep the populace as safe as possible. However it breaks down, whether it's the county or local community who calls the final shots, that's a politician's concern. A voting issue. I'm a firefighter."

"And an arson expert."

"Yes." His haunted expression took her back to Christmas, when he'd singlehandedly discovered the accelerant the Female Preacher Killer had placed in the loft of the Silver Valley Community Church just minutes after he'd arrived on scene. It'd been too late to stop the loft fire, but they'd saved every civilian present, including Zora and the organist. The civil action against Keith claimed he and his team had overlooked the accelerant during their inspection before any civilians had entered the building and thus endangered hundreds of churchgoers on Christmas Eve.

"I spoke with Detective Ortega today."

At his immediate silence and stony expression, Kayla cringed. She hated causing her brother any more angst. He'd had enough.

"And?" His face was unreadable.

"He thinks your case is tied in with something bigger that's going on in Silver Valley."

"He's right."

She jolted with surprise. "You already knew?"

"Yes. Rio came to me a week ago. He's done a lot of digging for me, and he's convinced I'm innocent. He was pretty much from the beginning, but he had to follow protocol. He's getting blowback from this single attorney who's come out of nowhere, with his clients insisting that I personally could have done something to prevent that psycho's actions. Rio thinks the couple has been hoodwinked by this lawyer. That he was out there looking for someone to file a claim against me and the fire department. It's pissing me off, Kayla, I have to tell you. First we all lived through the bastard's killing and stalking, then the fire. It's like he's still coming after us from beyond the grave."

"The janitor who was the Female Preacher Killer."

"Right."

So Rio had been watching out for Keith, even after they'd stopped seeing each other. He'd heard her when she'd spoken to him all those months ago. But he never mentioned it to her. Typical Rio—he allowed her to think the worst about him. She shook her head.

"What?" Keith didn't miss her motion. "It was the janitor who was the killer, the arsonist. My people couldn't have found his trap unless they'd had more time and been able to tear the balcony apart before the children's pageant."

"I'm not shaking my head at that. Of course I know that, and I believe you, Keith." Rio had believed Keith from the beginning, too, but she hadn't known it. "What I don't get is how can complete strangers keep you tied up in this bogus claim?"

Her younger brother flashed her a sarcastic grin. "Money, sis. Money talks and whoever it is wasn't happy when SVPD wanted all charges against me dropped. So they're coming after me with the civil suit. They're claiming that if we'd done our jobs correctly, the fire wouldn't have taken off so quickly. I'm lucky that SVPD is still trying to figure out why these civilians are so hell-bent on nailing me."

"You still think it's somehow your fault, don't you?"

"Hell, Kayla, there's always a part of me that feels responsible whenever anyone is hurt because of a fire. But no, I don't feel responsible for what that bastard did. And I have no doubt that I'll get out of this mess, but what I *do* doubt is that I'll do it before my career is completely shot."

She couldn't reply to his too-true statement. No matter how innocent he was, how untrue the claims against him and the department, the writing was on the firehouse wall.

If his case against him wasn't dropped soon, Keith wouldn't serve in Silver Valley's fire department again. Not without a lingering cloud of suspicion trailing him for the rest of his career.

"Have you thought about what else you can do?" She quietly heated up one of the casseroles she'd brought him in his microwave. He hadn't shaved in what looked like a week and he was in gym gear. At least the house was clean and he'd showered. "If you don't go back to the force?"

"No. Yes. I can become an arson investigator, maybe work for SVPD or go into the private sector. I've got other options, too, that have popped up. I just haven't explored them yet."

"Like what?"

"I can't say a lot about it, but there's an agency that

works covertly to solve crimes of all types. They contacted me."

"Here in Silver Valley?"

"No, not only here. All across the country, probably overseas, too. But my focus would be more local. To help out local LEA as needed."

"Are you talking about the CIA?" God, Keith wasn't thinking of anything so dangerous, was he? "Dad would have something to say about that." While in the Foreign Service their father had worked alongside the CIA in certain embassy tours and while he respected the agency it wasn't a line of work he'd ever want either of his children pursuing.

"It's not for Dad to say, just like it's not for you to tell Dad about this conversation. It's not CIA, Kayla. Just drop it."

"Fine." The microwave dinged. She pulled the hot dish out and lifted up the wax paper, releasing aromatic steam that she hoped her brother wouldn't be able to resist. "Here. Eat. You look like you're on a hunger strike."

"I feel like an outcast in my own damn town." Grumbling or not, he stood up and walked over to the stools at the high counter. "You're the best, sis. I appreciate it."

"It's the least I could do. You took care of me last fall."

"That was nothing." He shoved a huge forkful of food into his mouth. "Ouch! That's hot."

Blowing on his next forkful, Keith said, "You never told me who you were so upset about then."

"And I won't." She couldn't. If she told him about her brief, failed relationship with one SVPD cop, and then her disaster with Rio, he'd think she needed more than his help. That she was crazy.

Keith already had been through hell, having his stellar career yanked out from under him by the bogus claims. If he'd known he'd been the cause of her broken heart, no matter how indirectly, he'd feel even worse than he already did.

"Huh." He chewed, swallowed. "This is good stuff, sis. You'll make some dude happy with your wifely skills."

"Watch it or I'll make it hotter and make sure you can't talk to me like that."

"You're all talk, Kayla. You have a heart of gold and this food proves it."

Chapter 9

Soft footsteps startled Kayla, and the panic from last night threatened to make a full-blown return.

Rio stood in the middle of the shop, his athletic build and mesmerizing eyes proving an antidote to her anxiety. Not that she'd admit it.

"What are you doing here again?" She'd been working since returning to the shop after having left Keith's, and hadn't even heard Rio walk up to the front counter. She clicked on the appropriate commands to shut down the register computer and close the cash till before she allowed herself to look at him fully. "I thought I'd locked the front door."

It was a good thing the counter stood between them. She'd be lying to herself if she denied the thought of Keith's case being cleared up hadn't had her imagination going nonstop with images of what Rio and she had done together in bed, what they could do together again once he was no longer on the case.

"I told you I'm looking out for you. I wouldn't have asked you to keep an eye out for anything suspicious and then just left you on your own." He didn't have to spell it out for her. He'd appointed himself her security guard.

"So you got my text?" She'd told him she'd learned some interesting things at the Charbonneau house.

"Yes, but I don't want to talk about it here." He pointedly looked around the shop, with its huge front picture windows and artful displays that a customer could easily hide behind. "Come to dinner with me."

"That's not necessary. I'll close up and we can talk in the back like we did this morning." As soon as she said it, she stopped and stared at him. At his mouth, which was curving up to match the sexy glint in his eyes.

"That's what I'm talking about, Kayla. A public diner would be a better place, don't you think? Since we seem to get distracted in a more private setting."

"Oh. Okay, of course. I need two more minutes and we can go."

So he'd been as shaken by their kiss as she had. Good. If they both knew they needed to keep firm boundaries around their physical space, they'd stay out of trouble, right?

She clicked off the open sign and locked the front door before turning to Rio again. "Let's walk through the back and I'll lock up the receiving door."

"Right behind you."

That was the problem. She'd done okay and had even convinced herself that she was over Rio when she didn't have to see him every day. She'd stopped worrying about running into him randomly, for the most part.

But after last night, and the kiss this morning, things had changed. She was as tuned in to and turned on by Rio as she'd ever been. More, even.

She hoped they found Meredith's killer before she did something stupid, like convince herself that she'd made a mistake by shutting Rio out of her life.

"Are you sure you heard the word *florist* and not something else?" Rio's intense stare could make most people think twice even when they were sure, Kayla included.

"I'm positive. It's so obvious that they're involved. Do you think the mayor killed Meredith?"

"You tell me, Kayla. Did it sound like the mayor's voice that you heard yelling last night?"

"No. The mayor voice's isn't that deep. The killer, he was barely audible through the barn wall and door. I knew it was a man, I knew he was yelling, but it didn't carry as far. It was more of a roar, a vibration. I heard Meredith's voice and her screams." She stopped playing with the straw wrapper on the diner table.

Strong, dark hands covered hers. She forced herself to look at Rio.

"You okay?"

"I'm fine."

"*Fine* is one thing. *Okay*, quite another. It takes time

to digest the fact that you've survived a possible attempt on your life."

"No one tried to kill me, Rio."

"Trust me, he would have if he'd been able to. No murderer likes to leave the possibility of a witness behind. And he heard you."

"I may not have your training but I trust my common sense."

The waitress came up to them.

"BLT on rye—" she slid the platter in front of Kayla "—and a French dip." Rio smiled at her, his teeth flashing. Kayla watched as the waitress batted her eyes and gave Rio the once-over. "You all let me know if you need anything else, okay?"

Kayla ate a French fry as Rio replied. They'd never met over a meal before—their time together had been one shared beer at a community concert before they'd gone to bed. As cliché as it had sounded when she'd told him, she'd never had sex with a man on such short acquaintance and had let Rio know. He hadn't made the same declaration, but his touch had made her feel as if she was the first woman he'd ever laid hands on. His ability to bring her to multiple climaxes in one session had not been the work of a novice, though.

"I've had all my meals provided for today. First the coffee and croissant from you, then lunch at the Charbonneaus', now dinner. Not that I expect you to pay for this. I'm paying."

"It's on SVPD." Rio spoke with authority and she wasn't going to argue with him over a diner meal, but she knew "SVPD" meant her BLT was on Rio. SVPD was large enough but law enforcement didn't expense meals out with witnesses. She'd heard her brother complain about budget shortfalls in firefighting and suspected the police were no different.

"I've heard enough from Keith about budget shortfalls at the fire department. I'm sure it's the same for SVPD, right? I'm not taking money from your coffers, Rio."

"Back to your brother's case again, are we?"

"You should be more careful. You could be accused of bribing me with meals to keep me from putting pressure on you and SVPD to solve Keith's case. You know what makes me the angriest, Rio? You agree with me that Keith is innocent of all the charges that have been brought against him. But the investigation seems to have stalled since the civil suit was filed against him. I want to know why."

"We've done this dance, Kayla. And we're not talking about it."

"Yet you want me to help you out, help SVPD solve a crime. And you won't level with me on where you're at with Keith's case." She wasn't going to admit she'd found out just how much Rio was helping Keith. It would probably embarrass him, at the least, and anger him if he thought she was prying.

"I am helping Keith, Kayla. If he's innocent the facts will play out." His voice was low and angry.

"You don't get to question me about a case you're more interested in and leave my brother's career in the balance, Rio."

His lips thinned and he tapped the top of the leather

bench with his fingers, which gave away his inner turmoil. *Jackpot.*

"You're going to have to trust me on this, as much as you and I have difficulty with the concept."

"More like I'll never be able to trust anyone investigating my brother."

"Your brother's case is one of many on SVPD's plate. Of all people, anyone in law enforcement is the last person we want to incriminate, unless they've earned that scrutiny. You have to trust me on your brother's case, Kayla." His eyes remained fixed on her and she had to work at it to not blink or fidget or look away.

"Fine."

Rio kept up his stern demeanor for a few more beats before a lazy grin crept across his features.

"I knew you couldn't resist my charm."

"Shove it, Rio."

His laughter rumbled in their booth and broke the tension.

"How's your family doing, by the way? How have you been?" She didn't want to talk about the case anymore, at least not for a few minutes while they finished their meals.

"Nice change of subject." He stared over her shoulder as if he was solving a physics problem instead of thinking about his family. "They're all well. I would still love for you to meet them. My mother and stepfather stay busy with their small farm and grandkids, and my sisters still love trying to nose into my life when they have time amid all the parenting stuff. It's nice to see my parents finally relaxing. Dad retired last year, and he and Mom are talking about opening an authentic Tex-Mex restaurant."

"That would be a great addition to Silver Valley." There were a few Mexican restaurants in town but most were part of a chain.

"My sisters think they're crazy, but they aren't too old. They're only in their fifties. My sisters are both mother hens, with Mom and Dad and with me."

She remembered he was the only brother of three siblings. Just like Keith. "It's a sister's prerogative to keep tabs on her brother and his love life."

"They thought you might be the one for me."

She froze. "You told them about us?"

"Not in detail, no. That would be gross." He grinned while she squirmed, wanting to laugh at his joke but only finding herself able to remember the "details" Rio referred to.

Pathetic.

"You've gotten quiet again, Kayla."

"I just don't have anything to say on that subject."

"Fine. Then let's go over your events with Gloria again. This time, I want you to tell me how you felt while you talked to her, what you thought about the house."

"You want my emotions? That's a little touchy-feely for a cop, isn't it?"

"Indulge me." Rio dipped his fresh-baked bun, loaded with layers of thin-sliced beef, into a side bowl of jus. "Want a bite?" He held up the sandwich, his eyes warm and inviting.

"No, I'm good." Taking a bite of Rio's sandwich was too intimate, too close. The kind of thing they might be doing if he wasn't working on Keith's case. "Before I go on, can't you give me a nibble on what's happening with Keith? You know he's not guilty."

"I've told you over and over that I can't talk about it, Kayla. And this isn't tit for tat. You don't have that impression from me, do you?"

"No, not at all. But you can't blame me for trying." She sipped her water as she prepared to change tactics. "You asked me how I felt. Usually with Gloria I have the sense that she is looking down on me. That everyone exists to do her bidding. I only met her twice before, because her assistant, Sylvia, usually orders her flowers and when we deliver we leave them at the door because their front porch is covered. Today, Gloria seemed rattled. It wasn't anything you'd notice unless you were looking for it, but she wasn't as self-contained as normal."

"Go on."

"It's as if she's worried about something. And I noticed this before she took the call from her husband."

"He called on a burner phone, you mentioned."

"I think so, from what they said. And you know, I'm not in law enforcement, but why would anyone but a criminal need a burner phone?" She wondered why they even existed.

Rio shook his head. "Burners are a great thing for a tourist, or if your phone dies and you aren't up for a new one on your contract. Unfortunately they can also help people get away with a lot of bad behavior. But if it was the mayor and he called their home phone, or her office line if she has one, I'll be able to get the information I need."

"He said she'd given him a lot of them." She wanted to make sure he'd heard that part of her story.

Rio speared a fry. "No problem." There was more he wasn't sharing with her, she could tell by the way he set his jaw, but she didn't need to know the details of any of this. She just wanted to prove her brother was innocent, and if helping SVPD on this helped Keith, it was a small price.

"You can't tell me what you know, but can you tell me if I'm on the right track thinking that there's something bigger going on in Silver Valley?"

His eyes were shielded. "Bigger in what way?"

"I'm not blind, Rio. I was the one who delivered one of the bouquets from the Female Preacher Killer, remember?" She knew he hadn't forgotten. She'd unwittingly taken a death threat to the home of her good friend Zora Krasny. Soon-to-be Zora Campbell, since she was marrying SVPD detective Bryce Campbell. "And you and Bryce, you're close. I saw the two of you shopping together at the last-minute Christmas bazaar."

"Zora likes the brooch you helped Bryce pick out."

"I didn't help him—he knew what he wanted. Stop changing the subject. There's something going on—is it a drug ring? Is what happened with Mayor Donner and the quick election part of it? Is there more than money laundering going on?"

"Money laundering. That's a heavy charge."

"Spare me. It's on the SVPD blotter reports and

on their Facebook page. The crime rings out of Philadelphia, New York and Baltimore funnel new immigrants up through towns like ours to shop in the big-box stores. They purchase a television at two or three in the morning, with cash, and then when they return it with the receipt they get cash back. This time the cash is, in all probability, legit."

"Mmm." Rio sipped his water and waved down their waitress. "Can I please have a cup of coffee?" He looked at Kayla. "Would you like some?"

"No thanks, I'm good." She knew from Rio's overly calm demeanor that she was hitting pay dirt, but also understood that above all else, Rio was a professional. He wasn't about to tell her police business. Not unless she absolutely had to know to help them find Meredith's killer.

Her phone buzzed on the table and she looked at the ID. "It's Gloria. I can call her back later."

"Answer it." Rio's request was swift, sure. She picked up the phone and looked at him as she answered.

"Hi, Gloria. What can I do for you?"

"I'm terribly sorry to bother you for the second time in one day, Kayla, but there's an entire aspect of the wedding I forgot to go over with you."

"Oh?" She had six files of what Gloria expected for flowers on the wedding day, from the gazebo to the house to the front entryway. Bouquets for the attendants, a special bouquet for the bride to toss and an entire folder devoted to the bride's flowers. A full trailing bouquet of rare exotic blooms with an equally stunning floral headpiece. Kayla thought it was all a bit gaudy, but she was there to provide whatever Gloria and Cynthia wanted.

"Yes, we forgot to discuss the tables at the rehearsal dinner. We'll have it at the Serenity Inn in Amittstown, the same place as the reception the next day. Do you know the place?"

"Yes, I decorated for a bridal shower there last year." The dining room in the old Civil War-era farmhouse was small, but maybe they were keeping the rehearsal dinner more intimate. "Do you want more than a centerpiece?"

"Of course! There will be eight tables of eight for the rehearsal dinner—a quarter of the size of the wedding dinner. We'll need a centerpiece at each. I was thinking of a more masculine theme, and I have a great idea for the party favors. I was hoping you'd handle it all for me."

"Just let me know what I can do. Is there...?" She was about to ask if the groom's parents were participating and then remembered that there was a good chance that Judge Charles Blackwell's parents might not be living. The man had to be at least twenty years Cynthia's senior. "Is there anything in particular the groom would like? Would you like me to talk to him?"

"Oh, no. I know that customarily the groom handles the rehearsal dinner but we'll be doing it all for Charles and Cynthia. Charles's father is dead and his mother is in a nursing home so she won't be attending any of the events. Tony won't have anything less than the best for his daughter. For the favors I thought a tiny gavel with the date on it would be so cute, you know, since Charles is a judge."

"I'm sure I can find a miniature gavel on Etsy or perhaps more locally. Gloria, is there a price limit for the decorations for the rehearsal dinner?"

"Price?" Kayla imagined Gloria blinking her over-the-top false eyelashes, as if the question of price was never an issue. "No, no, of course not. I mean, how much could eight centerpieces cost? And the favors?" Kayla quickly did some numbers in her head and gave the figure to Gloria.

"That's fine, Kayla, thank you. Will you be going out to look at the inn?"

"I've already worked there, so no, I don't see a reason to."

"I really think you should meet me out there. I'd feel better about it. Or maybe I can convince Cynthia to delay going back to school and meet with all of us."

Kayla was feeling more and more threatened by Gloria's requests. She wondered if Gloria's plan all along had been to get Kayla to another remote place not unlike the Weddings and More Barn. Like someone had done with Meredith. She mentally shook her head. This had to be paranoia from witnessing Meredith's murder. She agreed on a time and ended the conversation.

"This is insane. Why bother with a rehearsal dinner for a short-notice wedding? And they're having both the rehearsal dinner and the reception at the Serenity Inn. Do you know it? It's forty minutes away. I have to drive from the rehearsal at the gazebo to the dinner, then do it again the next day for the wedding and reception." She spoke without considering her words. Anxiety gnawed at her.

"She's got you shaken up, hasn't she?" Rio's eyes were watchful and she wondered how he was able to read her mind.

"Why do I feel like I'm being stalked by her?"

"She thinks she's a powerful woman and she has a very strong personality. I doubt anyone's ever said no to her. Once she gets an idea going, she runs it into the ground."

She smiled at him. "That's the most negative I've heard you about anyone. You're usually more reserved. You certainly have an opinion about the mayor's wife."

Rio reached across the table and grasped her hand. She didn't pull it away.

"I have an opinion on most things, Kayla. I just don't feel a need to express it. It's not my job to have an opinion. My job is to keep Silver Valley safe and to see to it that anyone who tries to mess with that is brought to justice." As he spoke his thumb drew circles on her palm and she felt her desire hum to life.

She pulled her hand back. "It can't be like that again, Rio." She couldn't get intimate with Rio again and expect she'd survive breaking away like she had already done once.

"It won't be. It'll be different." She couldn't help the smile that his comment brought to her lips, but she stood up and grabbed her purse.

"I've got to get home. I'll wait outside while you pay the bill."

"You're not leaving my side, Kayla. Police procedure." She wasn't sure it was, but decided not to push him on it. If he thought she might be in some kind of danger, she'd listen to Rio. Just this once.

After Rio paid, they exited the diner and Kayla made a point of not looking anywhere in particular. She didn't want to make eye contact with anyone she might know. Her energy was low and she needed time to regroup.

Kayla had plenty of acquaintances in Silver Valley, more so since her business had gained traction over the past couple of years. In the main thoroughfare of the sprawling town, there was hardly a business she hadn't delivered to. From the strip malls to the upscale plazas, she'd taken flowers from one end of town to the other. Or had Jenny do it.

She really needed to look into hiring a full-time delivery person, or at least two part-time drivers.

"Ready?" Rio was next to her, his voice low in her ear. If she leaned in just a bit, he might kiss her on her earlobe, like he'd done when they'd made love.

"Sure. Let's go." It wasn't easy to follow him to the car and keep her mind off of how appealing his ass looked.

She was in trouble. Shouldn't she be more worried about getting through the Charbonneau wedding than fantasizing about a man she clearly needed to stay away from?

Rio killed the engine in her driveway and she was thankful when he sprang out of his seat and walked around to get her door before she had a chance to do it herself. At least, she told herself she was grateful. It wasn't as if she wanted him to turn to her in the dark confines of the car, reach across his armrest and...

"I want to make sure your house is clear, Kayla. Let me do this for you. Then I'll leave, I promise."

"You don't have to promise, Rio. I trust you."

"Maybe you shouldn't."

She ignored him and focused on getting her keys out instead. She placed them in Rio's outstretched hand and he let them both into the house.

"Stay here." She waited in the foyer as he disappeared into the kitchen and then upstairs. She heard the floorboards squeak under his feet, heard her closets open and close. She'd never admit it to him that it made her feel more secure to have him here. First witnessing a murder and then having to act as if she had no idea what was going on was wearing on her. She was a horticulturist, not an actor.

His sneakered feet appeared first on the stairs, followed by his long, lean legs in worn denim, stretched just tight enough across his crotch. His white shirt was next, and all she had to do was close her eyes and remember how flat and hard his abs were under that shirt, how his skin had heated under her fingers.

Judging from the expression on his face when he stepped onto the foyer floor, he remembered, too.

They stood no more than three feet apart with their eyes locked on each other. Kayla silently damned Rio's ability to get her so sexually aroused without a single touch.

"Rio." She didn't say more, couldn't. Because it

would be a lie to say anything denying her attraction to him. The heat that always simmered at the mere thought of him. The embers that ached to be blown into a full blaze again.

"Kayla, we agreed. We're friends." She watched his mouth shape the words and didn't miss the sardonic gleam in his eye.

"It's just like you to put it all back on me."

"It *is* on you. I would never have stopped seeing you."

"You had to."

"I don't have to do anything I don't want to, Kayla. I could have passed the case off to another officer."

They'd both taken a step closer and were no farther than a hand's width apart. Forced to look up at him, Kayla couldn't shake the memory of how he'd picked her up and carried her to her room. How they'd made love three times through a long Friday night, and after slow Saturday morning sex they'd had a king's breakfast of eggs, pancakes, bacon, melon and coffee. And then showered together before they'd made love again. In the shower.

"Stop reliving it in your head. I'm right here." Rio offered no further warning before he swooped in and kissed her, to which she offered absolutely no resistance. The kiss wasn't like the one in the flower shop. It had more intent. With this kiss, she was going to be back in Rio's bed, she knew. Well, *her* bed for tonight.

Rio would be damned if he'd let his mind take over and ruin this perfect time with Kayla. Their mutual heat was beyond attraction or lust. He wouldn't let himself call it more, especially that one four-letter word, but he'd call it a need.

Because he needed Kayla, needed to have her as much as he'd ever needed anything in his life. Her lips were soft but demanding under his. Dreams had been his only break from the long days of knowing there was a woman for him, yet he couldn't have her. Now the reality of being with Kayla again settled in and Rio knew how she liked it best. Hot and fast.

"Oh, yes, right here." She moved his hand under her shirt and over her breast, squeezing it with the amount of pressure she liked. Her hard nipple pressed against his palm and he took it between his fingers, teasing the taut flesh until she groaned again and he felt her sag against him.

Before he could grin at her sexy swoon, she'd cupped his balls through his jeans and did some squeezing of her own. Her fingers worked over him, undoing the top button on his fly, her skin touching his and making him see red.

He grasped her hands, his lips still on hers. Before he had a chance to think, he leaned down and kissed her on the curve of her neck, softly adding a nip with his front teeth. "Your bedroom, Kayla. Now."

She didn't answer him but kissed him back with fury, her breasts against his chest and her pelvis pressed against his erection. "Here, Rio. Right now." Kayla shrugged off her jacket, pulled her shirt over her head and shimmied out of her jeans in three seconds flat. If Rio wanted to make it to her bed with her, he couldn't. He needed her. Needed Kayla. He needed to be inside her.

"No fair." He threaded his fingers into her hair and cradled her head as he kissed her thoroughly, allowing his fingers to first unhook her bra and then meander south to her wetness, where he shoved two fingers inside.

"Rio!" Her cry drove him so close to climax he swore and withdrew his fingers, rushing to get out of his clothing. As he did, Kayla slipped off her panties and they stood facing each other at the base of the stairs, naked.

"Do you want me on the stairs, Rio?" Her pupils were dilated, her blond hair wild around her flushed cheeks, and her lips were swollen just like he loved them to be.

"Wherever you want me, baby." He watched her climb up two stairs before she turned and hitched a leg on his hip. He gave up on control as he lifted her and entered her in one swift stroke. They both groaned at the sheer pleasure of their joining, as if they'd been apart for decades instead of four months.

Kayla moved her hips over his erection and Rio helped her as long as he could. When he reached between them and touched her in the exact way he knew was her favorite, she screamed out. As she pulsed around him, he lowered her to the stairs and moved inside her without thinking. Only feeling, a rushing sense of knowing they fit together perfectly on every level, not just physically. He came hard in a crashing climax as Kayla cried out his name.

Chapter 10

Rio was summoned into Colt's office on Thursday morning. "Where are we on Keith Paruso's case?" Colt Todd eased back in his desk chair, his flinty eyes expectant as he looked at Rio.

"There's nothing new, and absolutely nothing against him, which is why I want to close the case. But not until I can prove the source of the accusations in the civil suit against him is one of the True Believers."

"Careful with that, Rio. We don't officially have a cult settling in Silver Valley—just some very suspicious people in a trailer park. Once it goes official, we have to call in the other agencies, and we're trying to avoid that for the moment. We need to let our friends in the background take care of it."

Rio knew Colt was talking about the Trail Hikers.

The two men stared at each other and Rio's stomach did a free fall before he clenched his fists at his sides. "And yet the True Believers have managed to sneak into our community, possibly get one mayor kicked out of office, keep the head of the fire department on administrative leave and now they're potentially tied to the murder of the mayor's assistant."

"You haven't found any hard links between the cult and Meredith's murder, have you?"

Rio shook his head, his exasperation building. "No, but it all makes sense. I just can't finger any one person. I don't have a murder weapon and we don't have any usable evidence. And there's the puzzle of the side door at the barn." He pushed away the twinge of guilt that tried to claw at his focus. Kayla didn't need to know about the possible second suspect, not until he was sure. He didn't want to worry her any further.

"It sounds as though the man who went after Kayla could have acted alone. But it's possible he didn't. Did Kayla mention any possibility of a third voice?"

"No." And Rio knew from experience that when your adrenaline was flowing it was often difficult to know exactly what you were hearing or seeing. If Kayla had heard a second female voice she could have easily mistaken it for Meredith's, and a second male for the killer's. "If Meredith had some dirt on the mayor or proof that the election was rigged, would it be enough to murder her? This is Silver Valley after all, not some big city."

Colt stretched his arms over and behind his head. "People have killed for less. And when you're in the political world, no matter what level, it can get myopic. It's not inconceivable that the mayor of Silver Valley has his eye on higher office. He wouldn't want anyone or anything to get in his way. Hell, he's spent more time with the governor and US Representatives to Congress than he has with me or any of the other community leaders in Silver Valley."

"He doesn't see you as a leader—he sees you as someone who works for him."

Colt snorted. "Yeah, he thinks I'm an hourly employee. At the first meeting we had, he asked how much I make per hour. He was stunned that I'm salaried. Not a political science whiz, that guy."

"How the hell did he get elected?"

"Your guess is as good as mine. But no matter how much we believe the money that got him elected may have come from the cult, or even that they might have rigged the election, we don't have any evidence." Colt's phone rang and he picked it up. "Todd here." Rio watched his expression. The man was a rock, and his rarely ruffled exterior didn't give Rio any insight into who the superintendent was talking to, or about what.

"Send her in." He hung up the phone and looked at Rio. "It's Claudia."

Rio knew Claudia as the Trail Hikers CEO. Rio admired her tenacity. She put safety first but always solved whatever crime the Trail Hikers had been brought in to help with.

A quick knock was followed by the appearance of the petite woman with knockout looks, silver hair included. She was old enough to be his mother but he never thought of her as remotely matronly. Her steady gaze skimmed over Rio before it settled on Colt.

"Superintendent. How are you, Colt?"

"Fine, fine. Nice to see you, Claudia. Please, have a seat."

Rio had stood and offered his hand to Claudia.

"Ma'am."

She shook it firmly while smiling at him. "It's Claudia, Rio. We've been through this."

"Yes, Claudia." He'd had a conversation with his closest buddy on the force, Bryce Campbell. They both found calling the former flag officer by her first name a bit uncomfortable as she'd probably seen more action in her career with the marines than either of them would ever see. She sat in the chair next to Rio and looked at him. "What's happening with the murder case?"

"I don't have anything concrete yet, but I do have some circumstantial evidence." He relayed what Kayla had told him.

"She's the florist from the Christmas delivery, from the Female Preacher Killer case." Claudia had the mind of someone half her age and her memory had never failed her while in Rio's presence.

"Yes."

Claudia nodded at his response, then turned toward Colt. "She'd be perfect to help with this. I can get some of my people inserted into the activity surrounding the wedding planning and ceremony, but as the florist she'll have the best opportunities to collect intelligence for us."

Rio didn't expect the sudden sense of his case spinning out of control that hit him. He felt as if he was in a kayak on the Susquehanna and hit with a surprise squall. "Kayla's one-hundred-percent civilian. She's already feeding us whatever she witnesses in the course of providing the floral services.

"How well do you know her, Rio?" Claudia's gaze didn't waver and his stomach did a double somersault. Shit. Claudia knew. That was the problem when you worked with government shadow agencies. They had the means to dig up the smallest details on people. People you cared about.

Like Kayla.

"I, uh, we dated. Very briefly." No way was he going to mention last night. "I had to end it when I was assigned to the SVFD case. She's the sister of the fire department superintendent. I was just telling Superintendent Todd that I haven't been able to prove any of the allegations against the fire chief."

"They're unfounded. I had two of my analysts examine the phone communications between him and the alleged persons he'd misdirected during the fire at the church. Fire Chief Paruso acted in the most exemplary manner and the charges need to be dropped. We can't help you with the civil suit against him, unfortunately."

A curl of excitement started in Rio's chest and went straight for his crotch. If the case was dropped, he could see Kayla again. If she'd agree to it. Judging by her defensive posturing after their lovemaking, he couldn't count on it.

But still.

"We have to make sure the press is informed and that any appearance of impropriety on his part is cleared." He looked at Claudia. "Can I see what your analysts came up with?"

Claudia nodded. "As part of the Trail Hikers, yes, you may. But you can't use our data publicly." He already knew that, but he'd be able to use their data to find something that could be released at an unclassified level.

"I won't. All I'll have to tell the press and the DA is that Paruso has been cleared. Remove all doubt, prove that he acted in the public's best interest before, during and after the Silver Valley Community Church's fire."

"Hold on, Rio. Claudia's right—you've got to make sure your testimony, and evidence, is rock-solid. The press will rip you apart if you have to say your source is classified."

"I'll make sure, boss. Claudia, can I head over to headquarters today or tomorrow?" Mentally he tried to see how he'd fit it in. He still had to interview the mayor and his daughter.

"I don't see why not. When you do, why don't you see if you can bring Kayla Paruso with you?"

Her words were as effective as a knife through Kevlar, cutting down the growing confidence he'd been feeling about Keith's case and his chance at a relationship with Kayla.

"I don't think it's a good idea to bring her in, Claudia. She's a florist, an artist. Her parents have worked for the State Department her entire life and she wanted something different than government service."

The silence after he stopped speaking unnerved him and he shot a quick glance at Colt, who was in the midst of exchanging a telling glance with Claudia.

"I'm not trying to protect her, for heaven's sake. She's an adult and can make up her own mind, of course." He felt like he did every time his mother had caught him sneaking a cookie out of the pantry. As if his hand held something that would get him in a lot of trouble. Falling for Kayla would cause problems he didn't have time for.

"Bring her in like Claudia asked, Rio. You can wait until you finish your interviews surrounding the murder and clear up Keith Paruso's issues, but then I want to hear from Claudia that Kayla has been read into the program."

"Colt's right, I'm sorry, Rio. I forgot that you have a lot on your plate. At any rate, have Kayla come in to the Trail Hikers office before next week. We'll need at least two solid days to make sure she's trained with a weapon and understands some basic self-defense."

"Will do." Hell, they were going to put a weapon in Kayla's hands? The hands that were adept at making art out of flowers and stems? The hands that had been on his...

"You're on your own until you find out more information about the Houseman case." Claudia gave him his last order for the time being. Rio nodded at each of his bosses and left the room, closing the door behind him.

Claudia only ever had conversations behind closed doors at SVPD.

* * *

"I don't have much time to be out here with you." Cynthia stood on the gazebo platform, appearing impatient and a bit bored. She'd made the twenty-minute drive from school specifically to see her stepmother and Kayla for the wedding planning. She'd told Kayla three times so far. Kayla had worked in the appointment even though it was the day before Good Friday and dozens of Easter orders loomed. Jenny was taking the load of the deliveries and shop business today.

Kayla kept taking photos of the gazebo from every angle with her phone, using a ruler to help her judge the scale when she was back in her studio. The flowers she needed were going to cost a small fortune, but with a virtually unlimited budget she'd make it happen.

"What are you measuring for, exactly? Didn't Gloria give you a copy of the gazebo's blueprint?"

"No, and it wouldn't help. I need to know how thick the railings are, what the light's like."

"That's brilliant. I would have never thought about the light."

"Hmm."

While talking to Cynthia might eventually yield a morsel of information, what Kayla really wanted to do was to get into Gloria's personal office, unseen. It wasn't going to be easy with Cynthia here, along with Sylvia and Gloria.

Rio had made it clear that she wasn't to do any snooping, but would simply observe things as they happened. Thinking of him only made her think of last night, of how carnal they'd been on the stairs and how she wished it could happen again. What happened to the intentions she'd had to stay away from him?

Being the good girl had never been her modus operandi.

"Are you going to be able to have it done in time?" Cynthia's voice grated across her nerves like sandpaper, dissolving her pleasant fantasy. Kayla was grateful that she was on her knees measuring the gazebo's railing, with both hands busy, or she'd have jumped at the sound. What was it about Cynthia's voice?

"Yes, no problem." She eased back to her feet, keeping a steady awareness of Cynthia's location.

"Gloria isn't so sure." Cynthia ran her long fingers over the wooden balustrade, her nails short and blunt, her long-sleeved blouse more fitting for a courtroom than this backyard. Gloria had meticulously designed it to look like the Borghese gardens in Rome. At least, that was what Kayla assumed she was doing with the tacky faux-marble statues dotting what had been a more natural landscape only a few months ago.

"I've promised her I'll deliver, and I'm promising you that, too. Don't worry about anything but enjoying your big day. I haven't backed out on a client yet." She tapped more notes into her smartphone, reminding herself to be generous with the green ivy. It was far too early in the season to be able to depend on the local nurseries; she'd have to order in from Virginia or even the Carolinas.

"It doesn't matter to me. Charles and I could just as well elope to Vegas or Mexico. But my father, he's old-fashioned."

"Hmm." Kayla couldn't look at Cynthia without risking her feelings being stamped on by her expression. If the mayor was so "old-fashioned," then why was he encouraging such an obviously strategic marriage?

"You don't approve, do you, Kayla?" Cynthia could have said *Who the hell do you think you are?* with the chill her tone blasted over Kayla.

"It's none of my business, Cynthia. My job is to provide you with the most beautiful flowers for your special day. I honestly don't have time to think past that."

"I wouldn't blame you." Cynthia tossed her hair. "If you didn't approve, that is. It is rather odd for someone like me to marry a man so much older and set in his ways. He doesn't want any more children, which most women my age wouldn't go for. But I don't need kids. I'll be too busy with my career."

"Practicing law can be all-consuming."

"Oh, I don't plan to stay in law for too long. My degree is a means to an end. I want to run for office."

"Locally, like your dad?"

A smile stretched over Cynthia's gaunt features, making her appear more like the Grinch than a young bride-to-be. "Who's to say? But I don't do anything without going for the top. You know, go big or go home."

"Yes, I heard you're the top of your class at law school."

Cynthia sniffed. "That's not important to me. My future, *our* future—" she smiled as she looked around the gazebo, presumably picturing the wedding ceremony "—that's what matters."

For the second time in as many days, Kayla was struck with a deep dislike for a woman she barely knew.

What was it about Cynthia Charbonneau?

"Are you absolutely sure she has no idea?"

Gloria could tell Mickey Ippolito was worried again. Familiar annoyance curled in her gut as Mickey questioned her for the umpteenth time.

"Honey buns, I'm sure," she said. "That girl only has eyes for her father and has no clue what's going on with us. Hell, her daddy doesn't suspect, why should she?" She watched him stare at the ceiling and ran her fingers over his nose, his lips. "You worry too much. You need to trust me on this, Mickey. And we need to start our life together. Why don't you let me leave him now?"

"I want to start our life together, too, Gloria. But it's not time yet."

"It's never time, Mickey."

"I told you it might take a while. He had to get settled and secure in this new job before you leave him. Before we both leave him. It's going to come as a huge shock to him."

"Do you really think so?"

"Oh, yeah." His calm demeanor masked a sneer.

"You're getting all tense again. Why don't you let me calm you down?" She tried to inflect a purr into her voice with no luck. She missed how their lovemaking used to be so endless and enjoyable. Recently it'd been perfunctory, which was a total bummer considering how much work it took to sneak around Silver

Valley in order to be together. "Sometimes you make me think he doesn't want to be with me. Has he said something to you, Mickey?"

"No, no. He's been the same at work."

"What has he had you do lately?" She hated to ask because she was concerned the answer might be her biggest fear: that Mickey had been the one to kill Meredith Houseman. Tony swore it was some kind of fluke that Meredith had been out at the barn where Gloria had booked the original reception at the same time as some crazy killer, and that of course he'd had nothing to do with Meredith's demise. He'd simply sent Meredith out to get information for the wedding. At least, that was what Tony told her.

Gloria believed Tony—he didn't have the balls to fire anyone on his staff, much less murder her. But if he'd thought Meredith had any dirt on him, he might have persuaded someone else to take care of her. But did he? And was it Mickey who'd done the dirty work?

"You don't think Tony had anything to do with Meredith, do you, Mickey?"

"I don't know, Gloria. The man seems clueless, but then he surprises me sometimes. I'm his assistant whenever he needs some dirty work done, but the rest of the time he treats me like garbage. He'd never expect I'd be the one to take away his gorgeous wife."

"Oh, Mickey, you make me feel so beautiful."

"You are beautiful, Gloria. And you deserve more than what that guy and his daughter are giving you. They treat you like their slave."

"Not for much longer."

"No."

They kissed slowly and Gloria couldn't help but smile against his mouth. She knew that Mickey would do whatever she wanted.

Kayla thought Cynthia would never leave. She could outwait the best of them but it was getting tiring as she pretended to keep measuring outside for the wedding flowers. She needed to get inside the house on her own and take a look around.

After Cynthia ended a brief phone call, she shot Kayla a satisfied smile. "That was my future husband. We're meeting for lunch. Are you almost finished out here?"

"I'm fine. I would like to use the restroom on my way out and then do a few measurements in the foyer."

Cynthia's forehead wrinkled with consternation, but it smoothed so quickly Kayla wondered if the woman ever let her emotions show.

"Okay, then. Do you mind letting yourself out when you're done?"

"No, not at all." Besides, wouldn't Gloria or her assistant be around? She tried to not act too eager. It would be a nice stroke of luck if she had a chance to look around the entire house on her own.

"I'll let Sylvia know you're still here on my way out."

Damn it.

"Thank you so much." She waited a five full minutes for Cynthia's departure before she reentered the house, her measuring tape held in front of her as a convenient alibi if anyone found her.

They probably have security cameras.

To cover her tracks, she took measurements of the entire foyer before she walked into Gloria's empty office. The house was still, as if everyone had left for the afternoon or had lunch dates. Gloria's desk was neat and orderly and her drawers locked. Kayla found nothing unusual, which wasn't surprising since she didn't even know what she was looking for. There was no sign of Sylvia, much to her relief.

Disappointment threatened to shorten her snooping, but before it did she left the office and measured the staircase. She only needed the balustrade's length, but took her time, climbing each step as quietly as possible. Fortunately the old house had been expertly renovated and the stair treads were solid and polished under her canvas flats.

At the landing she ventured a look outside and saw a view of the street. She sucked in a quick breath when she saw Cynthia standing next to a luxury sedan, her hand on the door handle as if to get into the car. She was speaking to a man Kayla didn't recognize. He appeared shorter than Cynthia and much wider. Kayla let out the breath she'd sucked in when Cynthia got into her car and drove away. The man walked toward the house.

When the front door opened without a knock, Kayla froze. Who was that man?

She looked up the short flight of remaining stairs to the second floor and saw a bathroom directly in front of her. Without hesitating she silently took the stairs and went into the small powder room, closing the door behind her.

This is silly. The man was probably a friend of the family's or one of the mayor's assistants.

Sure steps sounded on the stairs and Kayla had no doubt the man was on his way up here. What if he was a plumber and needed to look in the bathroom? She'd tell him she'd needed to use it while doing her job, that was all. Still, the pen in her hand slipped as her palms perspired. Hadn't the other night taught her that she was a florist, not a hero?

She got on her knees and peered under the crack between the door and deco-era tiled floor. Footsteps sounded on the hall runner and she watched his feet pass in front of the door. She held her breath until his feet disappeared.

"I wondered what took you so long." Gloria's voice carried from a nearby room with a sexy pout that didn't match her words. Kayla looked for the source of her voice and found a vent under the pedestal sink. She got on her knees and discovered it allowed her to look into the room on the other side of the wall, where Gloria had to be. Sure enough, the feet that had walked by the bathroom door were in view. The man kicked off his shoes and she made out a set of very hairy legs and quite ugly feet.

This was unexpected.

"It's worth the wait, isn't it?" The gruff male response hit a primal nerve that made Kayla jump, her head banging into the elbow pipe underneath the porcelain sink. Long seconds passed as she waited to see if they'd heard her. Instead, she heard the bedroom door close and the distinctive click of a lock.

That voice. It was the murderer, she was sure. The man from the barn. And he was about to get into bed with Gloria in her bedroom. The mayor's bedroom. *Wait—what if he is going to kill Gloria?*

Or what if she found out Gloria was in on the murder?

"I ran into Cynthia as she was leaving."

"Oh, my God, Mickey, we have to be more careful. What did she say?"

Mickey.

"Nothing. I told her I was stopping in to pick up something for Tony."

"Thank goodness. If she finds out…"

"Baby, don't worry. By the time either of them finds out, we'll be far away."

Silence, then the rustling of clothing or sheets, and the distinct sound of a belt buckle hitting the floor made Kayla cringe. She could hear everything so clearly through the vent. That meant they'd be able to hear her if she wasn't exceptionally quiet. She was lucky they'd been talking and hadn't heard her head bump.

She had to get out of here. It creeped her out that Gloria had been in the house and she hadn't known it.

She'd have to wait until they were in the heat of the moment. *Ugh.*

Gloria and "Mickey" didn't speak for a few minutes, but when their conversation grew louder and more graphic, Kayla knew that was her chance to get out unseen.

Making it back out into the hallway was the easy part, as the door opened without a problem and she praised whoever had greased the hinges. Mickey and Gloria were in full lovemaking as Kayla tiptoed down the stairs, her ears unable to catch their words. Whether from the distance between her and the bedroom, or the pounding of her heart, she didn't know or care. She had to get out of the house.

Once out on the front porch she let the sunshine hit her face full force and took a couple of deep breaths before she hightailed it up the sidewalk and the two blocks to the shop. If she'd parked the florist van in front of the house, Mickey would have seen it and he would've looked for her. Or been more careful.

She texted Rio, telling him everything she'd gleaned as she walked, and was grateful for the space to think before she had Rio grilling her over what she'd again heard.

Got it. Thanks. Stay away from trouble. Let's meet tomorrow. Lunch.

His reply confirmed he was knee-deep in the investigation and she knew that he'd meet sooner if he could. Still, the ache of disappointment in her chest was undeniable.

Chapter 11

On Good Friday Kayla was grateful to be able to immerse herself in the shop's heavy workload. It kept her mind from wandering back to the other night, the staircase and Rio's hands on her. Not that she was seeking any kind of forgiveness, despite the fact that this was Good Friday and Passover. That would make her a hypocrite, because she wasn't sorry for making love to Rio again. But it would be so much easier if she hadn't. If their chemistry had perished with the hope of a relationship.

Maybe your idea of what kind of man you see yourself with needs to change.

Not wanting to face the tough question, she turned to what had given her solace since high school. The flowers. She worked six hours straight before she took a break, right before noon.

"I'm going out for a quick lunch and a cup of coffee. Do you want anything?" Kayla had five minutes until she had to meet Rio at the coffee shop in the plaza across from the store.

Jenny shook her head. "No, no coffee, but could you bring me back a smoothie?"

Kayla grinned. "Sure thing. You still on your 'green smoothie with protein' kick?"

"No protein powder today. Just all green. Ask them to make it with the frozen yogurt, too, please."

"Will do." Kayla walked out the front door and waited at the curb for the heavy afternoon traffic to offer a clearing. As she walked across the street, she realized she, too, would love a smoothie. Maybe she'd convince Rio to make their coffee meet-up a trip to the juice bar instead.

She saw his sedan pull into the parking lot and hated the bolt of awareness that zinged through her body. The other night had been an exception for both of them. It had to be or they risked putting each other in danger— they were a distraction to each other.

She reached him as he stepped out and not for the first time she was mesmerized by how white his teeth were against his dark skin, his sunglasses shielding his eyes from her. He looked so damn sexy and sure of himself. Of course he did. He'd been quite the lover Wednesday night.

Damn it.

"Would you mind going to the juice bar instead? I

haven't had lunch yet and I was hoping for a smoothie. Jenny wants me to bring her back one, too."

"A smoothie. Okay." His tone indicated that he didn't think a smoothie would be enough sustenance, but she was already walking toward the popular spot, needing to put space between them. Rio caught up to her and she glared at him.

"Don't be so damn defensive, Kayla."

"I'm not being defensive."

He matched her stride, then reached out and opened the door to the café for her. "Sure you are. You're mad at yourself for the other night."

If she thought the bolt of attraction she'd felt at his appearance had been heady, it was nothing compared to the flash of heat that went through her now.

"Um, I believe it was mutual."

"Yes, it was." His smug concession allowed her to maintain at least a portion of her pride. He was a wonderful lover, yes, but he'd enjoyed it as much as she had.

"You're not making it easier for us to work together, Rio." She stared at him while he calmly perused the menu that was above the counter. Much to her chagrin he remained calm, pausing only to give her the briefest look.

"Let's get our order before we talk, shall we?"

She ordered a mango-ginger smoothie with extra ginger, while Rio settled on a strawberry-banana yogurt smoothie. "You're not a smoothie kind of guy, are you?"

"It's like dessert before lunch, but it works." They took seats at a small table in the corner. There were seats outside that Kayla enjoyed on nice days, but just like her shop, it was too risky to be out in the open and discussing anything about the case. No one needed to hear what they were talking about.

"What do you know that you didn't put in your text, Kayla?"

She told him again what she'd overheard while at the mayor's house, this time adding details and nuances her text didn't convey. Rio's expression remained passive until she paused.

"You never should have gone upstairs. Whatever possessed you to go into the bathroom?"

"I want to get to the bottom of this as much as you do, Rio. And I was already there. Once you hear everything I found out, you won't be so concerned about how I got it."

"I'm all yours."

Rio grinned at Kayla, hoping she wouldn't take his reply for anything more than a common expression. Because for one heartbeat, he'd meant it. He'd ask to be removed from her brother's case, do whatever it took to get Kayla back in his arms. And then he remembered—she didn't want to be in his arms, and he had no business trying to get her there.

"I was at the mayor's house to take measurements for the wedding. The gazebo, inside railings, wherever Gloria wants garland."

"And Cynthia was there early on?"

"Yes—in fact, she didn't want to leave me alone.

. It's clear that she was in charge of keeping an eye on me, for Gloria."

"You think they still suspect you know something?"

"Actually, no, I don't. Cynthia eventually left and I had a chance to walk around on my own." She went on and told him more of what had happened. He had a hard time keeping his expression neutral when she described being all but trapped in the bathroom with two potential criminals on the other side of the wall, but he stayed silent, not wanting to miss one iota of the facts as she relayed them.

"I was going to text you while I was in the bathroom but didn't want to waste any time. I had to get out of there as quickly as possible, and my, er, window of opportunity was small."

He laughed. "That is a very polite way to put it." He looked at her eyes and kept himself from caressing her cheek, her jawline. She'd acted like a pro.

"You're not in law enforcement, Kayla. I don't want you going into the Charbonneaus' house by yourself again. Take your assistant with you. Or better yet, call me and I'll escort you in and out."

"That's crazy. I'm not in danger there, am I?" The quaver in her voice told him that she knew better. He liked to make her voice tremble, but he'd rather do it in the bedroom. Protective instincts were part and parcel of being a cop, but when he was around Kayla his were on overdrive.

"Yes, I think you could be in a lot of danger. We don't know what we're going to find in this investigation. The motive for Meredith's murder is deeper than a personal conflict. By all accounts she and the mayor got along well." Except for some recent verbal exchanges that the mayor's receptionist mentioned overhearing. Kayla didn't need to know about that yet. "I need you to be more careful, Kayla."

"What was I supposed to do, Rio? The man I heard in that bedroom sounded exactly like the voice I heard in the barn. If I'd gone out the front door, or stayed on the stairs measuring, he would have seen me. He could have recognized me—he saw my shape when he chased me."

"Are you sure he chased you? Or was he running from the building, from the cops he knew were almost there?"

"I don't know. But I couldn't take a chance."

"Kayla, you did great. But again, you're not a cop. You aren't trained for the worst-case scenarios."

They sat without speaking for a bit, both lost in their own thoughts.

"You definitely heard them having sex?" His head tilted to the side, imperceptible to a stranger but not her.

"Yes." And it had been nothing like what she and Rio had done two nights ago. No sense of urgency. It had sounded...contrived, like a performance. But whether on Mickey's or Gloria's part, she didn't know.

Rio's frustration with her barely superseded his anger. Dark brows hadn't moved from their joined position in his troubled expression as he listened to her account of what she'd witnessed. Obviously he was worried about her safety.

"Do you know who Mickey is, Rio?"

"He's the mayor's assistant."

"Like Meredith was?"

Rio shook his head once. "No. Mickey's more of an operations assistant. Meredith was strictly administrative and a go-between for the mayor's staff and his accountant."

"Obviously Mickey's also a very personal assistant to Gloria." She thought her quip might coax Rio from his troubled emotions but she had no luck.

"You could have been killed, Kayla. If you're sure he's the voice you heard in the barn."

"I'm positive. But will recognizing a voice be enough for a court?"

"No. I need evidence. The bullets that killed Meredith were from a small pistol. I've already asked the mayor and his staff to provide any personal weapons they use, for the investigation. Mickey gave us his .45 and it's not a forensic match, nor is the mayor's."

"That doesn't mean anything. I mean, he simply used a different weapon, right?" She didn't want Rio to think she wasn't able to help.

"Right." Rio was curt, obviously annoyed with her. She knew she'd worried him with her latest escapade. Hell, she'd worried herself. But he was giving her a million-dollar reaction for a five-dollar offense. "What is it, Rio? What am I not seeing here? You look like you're ready to explode."

"There's some new evidence that I didn't want to cut you in on until the tech crew validated it. There's a high probability there was a second assailant that night.

He or she left through the barn door on the other side of the building from where Meredith was thrown."

"Impossible. I would have heard him."

"Unless they weren't talking. Or their voices were quiet. It could have been a woman, Kayla."

"You think it was Gloria? Helping out Tony or Mickey? Or both?"

Rio looked away, his concentration evident. "No, I don't think so. Gloria has an airtight alibi—Tony. And he has her for his alibi. They might not be on the best terms, but they're old-school when it comes to their professional dealings. They'll back each other to the end."

"Gloria might be the only one who realizes they aren't on good terms. He can't have a clue that she's screwing his close assistant. Speaking of whom, what about Mickey's alibi?"

"His alibi isn't as tight as theirs since he's single and lives alone, but his neighbors have corroborated that they saw him at home and in his yard around the time of the murder. He claims he went home for an early dinner that night and went to bed early. Says he fell asleep watching television by nine o'clock."

"That's impossible. I *know* it was his voice."

"Voices can sound similar. Especially a man's lower register, and you were in an extreme situation that night. Your adrenaline was flowing and you were trying to stay alive while figuring out how to help Meredith."

"I'm not crazy, Rio. It was the same voice."

"I trust you, Kayla, but we need harder evidence."

He'd said "we," not "I." Maybe he did consider her a partner of sorts.

"Short of a confession, without a murder weapon, will you ever get any?"

Rio sucked on his straw, the pink concoction half-gone. "I'm always hopeful."

She stared at Rio and knew he felt he needed to protect her from what he considered his territory. Their frenzied lovemaking had told her one thing if nothing else. That Rio still cared about her on some level.

"Rio, you're acting as if I did something you told me not to do. You're the one who asked me to find out what I could about Gloria and Cynthia."

"Not if it puts you in danger. I was specific about that." His eyes were bright and fierce. "You can't go into anything alone again."

"If I'd had Jennifer with me at the barn, we both might have been killed. We would have been talking and not noticed what was going on inside until we were right up on it. Have you thought of that?"

"I have."

"And yesterday if someone had been with me I would have never been able to sneak into the bathroom and get the information I did. It was a bizarre situation, I'll grant you, but it might yield more information at some point. As far as Gloria and Mickey are concerned, I'm the florist. If they'd seen me, all they would have worried about was that I'd figured out they were having an affair."

"That could be enough to get you killed, Kayla. The

mayor's history isn't the nicest, and we have to assume the same about the people closest to him."

"I know. I read the papers, see the news. It's clear to me that they're organized crime of some sort, and they barely escaped going to jail in New Jersey." She thought of the family summers they'd taken to the south Jersey shore when they were back on home leave and couldn't reconcile the peace and serenity of Stone Harbor, New Jersey, with the purported heavy crime syndicates that operated in the northern part of the state.

"Proof, show me some proof. Since the mayor and Mickey both have rap sheets, it's proof enough for me. They skirted the law their entire lives, and it's only by a hair that the mayor is legally eligible to run for elected office in any state."

"I still can't believe he got elected. And I want him out. This is my town, too, Rio, and I'm going to do whatever I need to do protect it."

"Leave the protecting to the cops, Kayla." He watched her. "Have you told me everything or is there something else?"

"No, I think that's it. Maybe it's time for you to tell *me* something, Rio?"

He dodged Kayla's piercing stare as he tried to convince himself the smoothie would fill him up. It was as if she had emotional X-ray vision around him.

Kayla was the only woman who'd ever forced him to look at his life and see what was missing. A family. A woman and not just a roll in the sack here and there. But Kayla deserved nothing less than a total commitment from him, and Rio had told himself for too long that he couldn't give anyone a total commitment, not with his job. But his other colleagues made marriages work. Maybe he needed to revisit his reticence. For Kayla it'd be worth the risk.

Not that she'd let him even come close to committing to her.

The idea that he'd never be able to reconcile his job with a family had been his reason to stay single until now. But that was before he met Kayla and had had not only the best physical relationship he'd ever experienced, but also the most mentally stimulating one, too. Kayla wasn't one to let life pass her by. She bit into it with all her teeth and left nothing untasted.

Rio couldn't break the classified parts of the case to Kayla, but she wasn't comprehending how dangerous her situation was, even with having witnessed a murder.

"About the night of the murder. I know you're certain the killer didn't see you, but you don't know that, not for sure. The fact that we didn't catch him concerns me. He could have circled back around or driven by and seen your van."

"But SVPD was there, Rio. You're telling me that they didn't check out each vehicle in the area?"

"Sure they did, once the murder scene was secured and they ascertained that you were okay." He watched her expression go from confident to cautiously optimistic to angry.

"You're telling me that all along I've been so sure

that SVPD had me taken care of that night and now you're saying there could be a gap in it all?"

"Yes."

She was quiet for a bit and he let her think. He was the same way. He needed his space to figure things out. It was one of the common traits they shared that had attracted him to her. Kayla wasn't one to blurt out whatever she was thinking. Her responses were always measured, considered. It was no doubt a key to her success as a florist, with the wide range of situations and emotional states the people she dealt with were in.

Kayla shook her head. "No, there's no way someone saw my van. I parked so far down the drive. We've been over this."

"We have, but that was before we confirmed that the side door of the barn across from you was ajar. There's a possibility there was a third person in the barn."

"And he or she didn't run into the fields behind the barn like the man who heard me."

"Until we prove it didn't happen, we'll assume it did. Have you picked up on anything questionable in your shop since this morning?"

"No. Jenny and I have been working nonstop since this morning. Gloria hasn't called me with anything other than a few orders that had last-minute changes."

"Okay. Now I need to tell you something about what's happening with Keith that might relate to Meredith's case. You know how sketchy the circumstances of Mayor Donner's indictment were? Well, I think the same group of people may be behind the accusations against Keith."

"Go on."

He pulled out his phone, where he kept his notes, and used them to make sure he didn't miss anything he felt she needed to know. Because Kayla needed to know about the True Believers. If he didn't tell her, he'd never forgive himself if she didn't take the threat against her seriously.

"Several members of a former cult that formed in upstate New York thirty years ago were released from prison over the past six months or so. For reasons that I can't go into right now, and more that I don't even know about, they've decided to settle in Silver Valley. The ringleader found a beneficiary who helped him purchase the entire trailer park community on the eastern outskirts of town."

"Cozy Acres Trailer Park?" She was alert, her eyes sparkling with interest. It was heady, having Kayla hang on to his words. He wanted her to hang on to his body with the same intensity.

"Yes, that's the one. You know it?"

"I've taken some floral orders from them. I only know it because the caller ID comes up when they call the shop. I didn't think there was anything odd about it because unlike the Female Preacher Killer last Christmas, they didn't use untraceable means to order flowers. They did what everyone else does. They called me."

"They might be fine, Kayla. Not everyone in that trailer park is a former True Believer, even though a former member appears to have used a front man to purchase the entire property."

"A True Believer?"

He sighed. None of this had made the press when SVPD had caught the Female Preacher Killer last December. For good reason. Superintendent Todd had been explicit that nothing to do with the cult could hit the media. They had to protect the ongoing investigation that the Trail Hikers were conducting into the True Believers.

"The True Believers were run by a man named Leonard Wise, who we haven't seen in Silver Valley yet, but we expect he'll show up down here. He served his term in New York and was granted permission to serve his probation here. So far, three of his cronies have shown up and live here. They haven't done anything openly illegal, but people like them, who used to hold women and children under their control with brainwashing and abuse, don't change."

"Was it a religious cult?"

"Oh, yes. With Wise as the ringleader. He impregnated girls once they were seventeen, after choosing them by the age of twelve to be the mothers of future True Believers."

"How the hell did someone like him ever get out of prison?" Her frustration echoed his.

"He wasn't convicted on every charge that he should have been. It's a hard crime to prove, since the girls were over the age of consent when he had sex with them."

"You mean raped them."

"Yes."

"And you're telling me about this why? Do you think

this cult had something to do with Meredith's murder? And what can I do about it besides listen and observe and let you know what I see?"

"I'm telling you for a couple of reasons. First, I want you to know that I'm not blowing smoke when I tell you to be careful and don't fight me on the extra SVPD patrols around your shop and house. Your safety is paramount. With this cult in town, anything is possible. Second, I have reason to believe that one of Wise's cronies is the lawyer who represents the family from Silver Valley Community Church who pressed charges against SVFD initially, and now Keith."

"I read in the paper that the family was new to the area, poor and felt disenfranchised by the church community." Kayla didn't miss one clue.

"Yes. Which made them ripe for picking when some sleazy lawyer cajoled them into filing charges against your brother. The charges against SVFD wouldn't hold and the lawyer knew it, so he recruited these folks."

"So all we have to do, all I have to do, is talk to this family and get them to reverse their accusations."

"No, you're not going to talk to anyone. I've got this. I'm meeting with the lawyer and family tomorrow afternoon."

"You work on Saturdays, too? You'll be doing that while I'm at the inn working on the wedding planning."

"I want you to stay in touch with me the entire time, Kayla. Text me when you get there, when you leave and every thirty minutes in between."

"Why don't I just take an SVPD car and drive myself there in that?" She tried to be sarcastic but he saw that he'd gotten through to her. Finally, the brave woman he cared about realized her life could be in jeopardy.

"Where will you be for the rest of the day?"

"At the shop. I have to place orders for the wedding, along with my usual orders. I've got a bit of a break since the holiday rush is over and we're still early for the wedding season."

He nodded.

"I want you to call or text me before you close up. Either I or an SVPD unit will follow you home."

"Rio, that's not necessary. No one has seen me— I'm the one they should be afraid of." She smiled and hoped it would coax a smile from him, too.

He looked at his watch. "We both need to get going. I'll expect to hear from you whenever you change locations, Kayla."

After they said their goodbyes, she went back into the café and ordered Jenny's smoothie. She wished all she had to worry about was how Jenny liked her drink, instead of figuring out how she was going to avoid getting shot during the next few days.

"This isn't what I'd planned for my term as mayor. I can't trust Mickey anymore. He was supposed to persuade Meredith not to do anything foolish. Not freakin' kill her."

"But, Daddy, he told you he didn't kill her. He said that he just roughed her up. Isn't it possible some crook came by and robbed her? There weren't any witnesses, right? There's no way we'll ever know what really happened."

"Men like Mickey can get worked up and do stupid things."

"Still, she deserved it if she was sticking her nose in where it didn't belong. Her job was to keep your schedule running, fend off the sharks, keep the appearance of complete professionalism from your office."

"She didn't deserve to die, Cynthia."

She laughed, very pleased with the tinkles of glee she'd perfected in front of her mirror. "I didn't mean that she deserved to die, Daddy. Just get a little shaken up by Mickey. Do you believe him? That he didn't kill her?"

"Of course I don't. He's protecting me and the office. Right now he swears there's no proof he was there, and if that's true, it'll die down. I have to trust that he didn't leave a murder weapon behind and that if he had one, it's long gone."

"Or at the bottom of the Susquehanna."

"You're my kid, Cynthia, I'll give you that."

Chapter 12

Saturday morning Rio walked up to the Sneads' trailer. The memories of being in the trailer park with Detective Bryce Campbell a few months ago when they'd been hunting the Female Preacher Killer flashed across his mind. The park had seemed mostly deserted then, but now he noted several more of the drab trailers had signs of inhabitants. Boots on the door stoops, flowerpots, a dog or two barking as he walked from his car to the trailer where the Sneads lived.

He was greeted at the door by a man he'd met before. The man had been with the guy who'd refused to tell Rio and Bryce where a missing girl was.

"Detective Ortega. I'm Justin Lacey, the Sneads' attorney." He held out his hand, which Rio shook.

"Haven't we met before?" Justin had been wearing

a flannel shirt and his hair had been closely cropped in December. Now it was longer, slicked back, and he wore a cheap suit that was too big on his scrawny frame.

"I don't think so, Detective." Rio wondered if the creep was trying to provoke him or was stupid enough to think Rio would believe him.

"I think we have. In December. You were here when I was with a colleague looking for a missing teenager."

A spark Rio could only describe as wariness flared in the lawyer's eyes. "You may be right. I've made a few friends in this area over the past few months. Not everyone can afford a slick lawyer and expensive fees. I'm happy to take on cases from people in hard times."

Rio figured Lacey's cases amounted to little more than ambulance chasing, but he kept his opinion to himself. He could see the Snead family sitting on their sofa over Justin's shoulder. "May I come in?"

"Of course."

Rio sat in an easy chair across from Bill and Barbara Snead. Justin sat at the kitchen counter on a stool, a yellow legal pad at his elbow.

"I'm here to find out what exactly you think you saw the night of the fire at Silver Valley Community Church, and to ask why you still believe it's necessary to press charges against the chief of the Silver Valley Fire Department."

"We're not pressing charges against one person, Detective. It's the whole fire department, because they didn't see what was coming." Bill spoke with a sense of bravado Rio didn't find impressive.

"My clients almost lost their lives that night. If not for the grace of God, they wouldn't be here to discuss this with you, Detective."

"Mr. and Mrs. Snead, if the SVFD hadn't done their job in the outstanding fashion they did, many people could have lost their lives. As it is, no one died and few were injured, even minimally. I'm asking you to look in your hearts and realize you're ruining the life and reputation of one of Silver Valley's finest citizens. Keith Paruso is a firefighter and leader we need. He doesn't deserve this hurtful charge you've filed against him."

"You don't have to answer that, Bill and Barbara. May I remind you, Detective, that my clients have agreed to see you? They don't have to talk to you or anyone on the Silver Valley payroll."

"Actually, they do. If you have witnessed something you're not reporting about the fire or that night, I need it for my investigation." He ignored Justin and addressed the Sneads.

Bill Snead remained steadfast in his indignant expression, but Rio saw the slight tremor of Barbara Snead's lower lip.

"Mrs. Snead, is there something you need to say? You understand that public safety is what we're talking about, not just your safety. If you know something I need to know, please tell me."

"I don't know..." She pulled a tissue out of the sleeve of her sweatshirt, which was printed with flowers and birds, and wiped her eyes.

"Just be quiet, Barb. We already told the police what

we know and no one listened." Bill Snead faced Rio. "Now people are listening."

"Barbara?" Rio stayed focused on the weak link.

"I can't do this, Bill." Barbara Snead blew her nose loudly before she looked at the floor and spoke. "We've been having a hard time since our kids moved out west. When we decided to sell our house, we never knew it would go so fast. But we owed so much and needed a place to live for a short time. We moved here and that's when we met Justin, who's been so nice." She looked at Justin, who was looking at his legal pad. "You're just doing your job, son, but I can't keep up this fight. I don't believe in it. Bill, this isn't who we are."

"Barbara, we've been through this. We're representing the churchgoers who could have been killed in that fire!"

"But they weren't killed, Bill. We weren't killed. We're right here. And as much as we need the money, I can't take money when we made it out of that burning building. No one else from church is filing any charges, just us. Don't you think that says something?" She looked at Rio. "I think the fire chief is the one who helped me out. And I know it's not his fault that no one knew about the gas bomb that the murderer had planted. I can't have it on my conscience that we ruined a young man's life, just because we were scared for a few hours."

"So you'll drop your accusations?" Rio didn't allow any sense of relief to grab hold, not yet.

"Wait a minute, here." Justin was watching a chance at a good chunk of money evaporate and it obviously wasn't his best professional moment. "You two were certain you needed to do this. Remember, it's not about you, but the whole church community. They were all put at risk unnecessarily. It's about keeping Silver Valley safe."

"We're dropping our claims, Detective. Mr. Lacey, we're sorry but we can't continue to work with you." Looking at his wife, Bill Snead spoke for them both.

"You have no idea who you're dealing with, Detective Ortega." Justin's bland face turned lethal as he spat the words. "This is bigger than you, bigger than the Sneads, bigger than Silver Valley Community Church. Certainly bigger than your local police force!"

Satisfaction curled in Rio's belly. He'd so obviously hit pay dirt. But Justin's reaction wasn't his concern; the Sneads were. They were whispering to each other and he hoped they'd woken up to the fact that they'd been bamboozled by this sleazebag.

Because Silver Valley needed to work together to get rid of people like Justin Lacey, a True Believer front man. It wasn't just about Rio being able to tell Kayla her brother was cleared of any wrongdoing, either. But if it helped her see that he was on her side, and was willing to change his job description to make her more comfortable with him, it had to be a good thing.

But is it enough to win Kayla's heart?

Saturday morning Kayla drove the van into the parking lot next to an old inn in a remote area of Central Pennsylvania almost an hour south of Silver Valley. The drive through the budding apple orchards didn't soothe her spirit as it usually did. She was as tense as ever. Helping out Rio and SVPD wasn't the problem. It was wondering if her motives were right. Of course she wanted to help clear Keith of the charges that were wrongfully stacked upon him. But was that all?

You want Rio free to be with you.

It was only natural, right? Rio was the hottest thing going in Silver Valley. She'd dated plenty but no one had impressed her enough to consider giving up being single, or committing to anything more than casual companionship.

She'd been brought up with an international sensibility that at times left her feeling out of step with the locals. Silver Valley had been her home for almost ten years, since she'd graduated college. In a town of over twenty thousand she'd never met a man as sexy or attractive as Rio. Or as stubborn.

Grabbing her iPad and phone, she swung out of the van and looked up at the refurbished Serenity Inn. Built before the Civil War, it had additions from the Victorian era and a modern addition that was a few years old. Kayla had done two or three wedding receptions here and one celebration-of-life dinner. She did her own designs and decorations when the client's budget allowed and the Serenity Inn was one of her favorites. As it was so far from Silver Valley, she didn't get many jobs down this way.

The front door opened with ease and she was grateful for the modernization that had added air-conditioning. The day was unusually warm and the humidity a killer.

"Hello?" Since it was before lunchtime, the restaurant area was empty as she wound her way through to the back catering rooms.

"Oh, hey, you must be the florist. Gloria told us you'd be coming. I'm Molly." A short woman with beautiful black hair down to her waist greeted her with a smile. "I'm the events manager."

"Nice to see you again, Molly. I'm Kayla. I remember you from when I worked a previous event."

"Yes, now I remember. I'm sorry, we have so many things going on here. Didn't you help out with the Mc-Crumb funeral?"

"Yes."

"That was something else. Your arrangements were stunning."

"Thank you. It was an honor." It was always an honor no matter the budget, but the McCrumb family had spared no expense for the matriarch of their clan when she'd passed at one hundred and three. Letitia McCrumb's passion had been roses, so it had been particularly challenging finding the right mix of blooms in the middle of January, when she'd died last year, but Kayla had been delighted to do so.

"Well, Gloria should be here soon, along with the caterer. Would you like something to drink while you're waiting?"

"No, no, I'm fine." Gloria hadn't mentioned that Veronique was coming, but it was probably smart. Flowers and food needed to coordinate, too.

"Okay, then, feel free to look around and brainstorm as needed. We'll all sit down once Gloria gets here." Molly walked out of the room and Kayla took

in her surroundings. She hadn't been in this particular room at the inn. The other events she'd handled
had been smaller than the Charbonneau wedding was
shaping up to be.

Deep walnut wainscoting ran the perimeter of the
long rectangular space. A banquet table sat in front of
a huge antique tapestry that she'd bet was Belgian and
very, very precious. She wrote notes about the main
centerpiece and then counted the round tables in the
room, thirty-two in all. Each seated eight and with the
head table, there'd be over two hundred and fifty guests
for the wedding dinner, a fraction of the rehearsal dinner number. She didn't need the exact numbers, but
Rio might. Kayla pulled out her phone and took several snapshots of the room to include the entrances and
exits. More information for SVPD.

"Why on earth would you need a photograph of
that door?" Gloria's query sounded right behind her
and Kayla had to fight to maintain hold of her phone.
Because of its large screen, Gloria had seen what she'd
taken a photo of.

"I thought you might want a garland around it, to
make it less utilitarian in appearance." She turned and
found Gloria towering above her in patent red pumps
and a zebra-print zip-front dress with a red patent
belt. The woman's hair was teased to within an inch
of cracking from the weight of the hair spray.

"Anyway, it's nice to see you, Gloria. How was your
drive?"

Gloria waved her question away. "Fine, fine." No
doubt every drive in her Mercedes was "fine." "But I'm

stressed to say the least. Cynthia is insistent that she can't move the wedding back any further and I have no idea how we're going to pull this off in a week."

"I've planned weddings with far less time. And it's nice that you're having both the rehearsal dinner and wedding reception in the same place." Her other short-notice weddings had been smaller, more intimate affairs, but Gloria didn't need to know that. "It'll all work out. Is something in particular bothering you?"

"All of it. I hate having to rush a social function of any kind. I'm a detail person."

"We'll make it work. Is Sylvia coming today?"

"No, she's manning the office for me." Kayla noted that Gloria treated her position as the mayoral spouse as its own entity. If she were a governor's wife, or the First Lady, it would make more sense. But Gloria didn't seem to do much besides run social functions for the mayor. And screw his assistant.

"Here you go." Molly walked in with a slender woman next to her. Kayla immediately recognized Veronique, the chef.

"Kayla, nice to see you again."

"Hello, Veronique." During the previous event Kayla had worked with Veronique, she had been all sweetness during the planning phase, but turned into quite the witch during the actual production. When Kayla had brought the flowers in for the celebration-of-life dinner, she'd witnessed Veronique chewing out her sous chef to the point of tears, all because the onions for a sauce had been chopped instead of minced. Kayla didn't consider herself a gourmet cook, but she knew her way around the kitchen and had helped her mother entertain large groups of diplomats. It was hardly ever important enough to fuss over such a small mistake in the kitchen. People came together to enjoy each other's company and rarely remembered what they ate unless it was exceptionally good or horrifically bad.

"Fine, let's sit down, shall we?" Molly gestured to the closest round table and they all took their seats. Gloria made sure her phone was in front of her and Veronique pulled out a huge leather binder.

"I have photographs for the menu selections." She handed the book to Gloria, who opened it and started turning pages.

"I like the idea of surf and turf. We'll please all of our guests."

Veronique cleared her throat. "It is more costly, I have to tell you. A buffet line would be best at this short notice. You can't be sure to hear back from everyone in time for a sit-down affair, and with the buffet setup we can do a few more dishes, and alternative desserts to the cake, to include gluten-free."

"Oh, but the cake is going to need to be gluten-free, didn't I already tell you that?" Gloria cocked her head in a practiced innocence.

Veronique puckered her lips as her fingers flew over her phone. "I do have that you asked for a gluten-free alternative…"

"The wedding cake must be gluten-free. That's non-negotiable. That way all of our friends can enjoy it. So many are gluten-free these days."

"Any other food allergies I should be aware of?" Veronique was a professional and Kayla gave her credit. Gloria wasn't the easiest client by far.

And now that she knew Gloria was also possibly a coconspirator to murder and cheating on her husband, Kayla found her presence nauseating.

"Are you paying attention, Kayla? Because the flowers are going to have to complement the courses." Gloria's brown eyes sparked with decisiveness and her perfectly manicured hands were folded in front of her. She'd tired of Veronique's book.

"Yes, got it." Kayla looked at Veronique and waited until they made eye contact. "You and I can work together to make it happen."

"Yes, of course." With an insouciant Gallic shrug, Veronique gave the impression of unflappability.

Kayla felt as though her blood pressure was spiking and wondered what Molly would do if she pounded her fist on the table.

"Things always seem overwhelming at the planning stage, don't they? But I promise, once the day arrives it'll go like clockwork." Molly had to be a middle child considering how well she smoothed things over. "I'll have my usual full staff of five along with six extras. We will all pitch in to make your daughter's wedding reception the most beautiful occasion."

"Cynthia's a tough girl to please. Trust me on that." Gloria sniffed, her patience obviously thin.

"Cynthia was excited about the plans I've drawn up for the gazebo. Why don't I bring them into the decor here? Veronique and I will make sure the courses coordinate." Kayla noticed that Molly had gone quiet, allowing her and Veronique to handle Gloria. She didn't blame her.

"It's the other way around, of course. The food first, then coordinate the flowers." Veronique was showing a tiny sliver of the electric-eel part of her personality that Kayla had seen before.

"You two work it out, I don't care how. I'm certainly paying you enough to do so." Gloria's hands shook as she read something off her phone, her lips drawn in a tight thin line reminiscent of Cynthia's persnickety attitudes. They might not be blood but the similarity was stunning. Kayla wondered what Tony Charbonneau's first wife—Cynthia's mother—looked like. Maybe an older version of Gloria? Mayor Charbonneau seemed to have a penchant for uptight, controlling women in his life.

"Back to your original question on allergies, Veronique. There are to be no scallops anywhere in sight of the meal."

"We're preparing lobster tails. Is that okay? They're both shellfish."

Gloria shook her head. "I'm only allergic to scallops. Lobster is fine, and one of my favorites. Although it's awfully messy for a wedding."

"No worries. My team and I will have them all split and ready to eat. No one will be cracking lobster shells at Cynthia Charbonneau's wedding." She gave a little flip with her hands, and combined with her French accent it made everyone laugh, albeit nervously. "I also thought it would be nice to have a seafood risotto on the brunch buffet table at your home, for immediately after the service. I plan to use shrimp and crab for that."

"That's lovely."

They sat and discussed colors and theme for the next forty minutes. Kayla would have excused herself, as Veronique had, when the conversation began to focus exclusively on the inn and what it was providing for the reception, but she thought better of it. She might catch a few extra morsels of information by staying.

Chapter 13

"I'd feel a little better if I could talk to Cynthia one more time before I go ahead with my orders for the wedding." Kayla knew it wasn't what Gloria wanted to hear, but Cynthia was a woman with a mind of her own and she had no desire to entertain headaches where she could just as well prevent them.

"I'm the mother of the bride. Shouldn't the final decision be left to me?" Gloria's overly made-up face puckered in a pout. Kayla wasn't going to be the one to point out that Gloria was at least twenty years younger than most mothers of the bride. She was probably not much older than Cynthia. Or herself, for that matter.

"Since Cynthia's the bride, I'd like to speak to her. It doesn't have to be today, but I'd like to touch base with her before tomorrow afternoon." Kayla had to have the specialty flowers ordered online by then so that her supplier could place the order first thing Monday morning. Her supplier was flexible and great to work with and she wanted to keep it that way. Changing a huge order like this, so short-notice already, was trouble for everyone.

"I'll tell her but she won't be back in town until late next week. She's back at law school."

Again, Kayla kept her mouth shut. How hard would it be for Cynthia to call her or drive the short distance to confirm details? But did Cynthia really want to get married? It almost seemed to be an afterthought.

You're making a good profit from this. Let it go.

But it wasn't about the profit. Kayla prided herself on her professionalism, and being forced to plan such a lavish wedding six days out was crazy enough without the bride here to add another demanding client.

Gloria looked exasperated as she shoved her planning calendar, lipstick—which she'd reapplied no less than three times in the two hours they'd had the meeting—and phone back into her expensive designer bag. "You're the florist, Kayla." Was that supposed to keep her in her place? "How different would Cynthia want it? She's trusted me with all the planning and I'm happy to do it for her. It's the least I can do for her and her father. They mean the world to me."

Sure they do. That's why you're doing the horizontal chicken dance with Mickey.

"Okay, well, if anything changes or you come up with any other ideas you'd like implemented, don't hesitate to call me. Cynthia, too, please make sure she has my number."

"Will do." Gloria's spiked heels clicked against the parquet flooring. The soles were lacquer red, of course. Nothing less than Christian Louboutin for Gloria.

Kayla waited to leave, taking a few extra minutes to look around the main reception room once more, visualizing where she'd place her arrangements and which colors and shades would do best in the subdued lighting. It was going to be an evening affair and Cynthia was adamant she wanted candles. But the fire codes limited their number.

She texted Rio and let him know she was on her way home. She'd call Jenny from the van once she was on the road. Hefting her tote onto her shoulder, she headed for the back door, closest to the parking lot. The door opened easily and she stepped onto a wheelchair ramp. She was pleased with the inn and all that it offered. It truly was one-stop event shopping. She also appreciated that while Gloria could have come here and had the inn provide everything from the food to the flowers, she'd stayed local to Silver Valley and the metropolitan area of Harrisburg. The gesture kept people like Kayla and Veronique in business.

It had rained while she was inside and she sidestepped puddles in the parking lot, noting that the clouds were still low, promising more rain. Raindrops glistened on the broad leaves of the shrubbery that was waking up after its long winter nap and she enjoyed the fresh scent of earth and sprouting fauna unique to spring. The parking area was surrounded by carefully pruned hedges that were taller than she was. She did a quick scan to make sure she was alone. The lot was empty save for her vehicle, which made sense as tonight's event probably wasn't until dinnertime, two hours away. Still, her hackles went up at how isolated it seemed, just around back from the small town's main street. She'd have to tell Rio that his warnings had finally sunk in. She imagined the bogeyman behind every corner.

Rio hadn't replied to her text yet. She knew she shouldn't look forward to anything from Rio except the safety he and the SVPD were providing her. But after their complete lack of self-control had led to the most spectacular sex, she'd thought of little else. Except for the murder of Meredith.

As she neared the van, she clicked the key fob in her hand and heard the loud *snap* of the locks and saw the rear lights wink on and off. The familiarity of the normal, everyday action didn't soothe her anxiety, though. She still felt the weight of the past week on her.

The same sound she'd heard for the first time only several days ago reached her ears a nanosecond before she felt something whiz by her ear.

A gunshot. *A bullet.*

She dropped to the gravel and dialed 911. Fast footsteps sounded on the gravel, footsteps Kayla hoped never reached her as she threw herself into the bottom of the arborvitae hedge. She scratched and clawed at the lower branches as she worked her way on her stomach into the middle of the border until she was safely hidden from view.

She needn't have worried as the shooter never appeared and she heard fast footfalls on the gravel, moving away from her.

"What's your emergency?" The dispatcher's request cut through her fear and disbelief.

"I've been shot at. I'm at the Serenity Inn in Amittstown. Please tell Detective Ortega at Silver Valley PD. It might be related to a case he's working on."

"Are you injured, ma'am?"

Dazed, Kayla reached for her ear. Her hand came away wet and in the dim light under the bushes she made out a red hue.

"Yes, but I don't think it's a big deal."

As she allowed the EMTs to tend to what they deemed was a minor abrasion due to being grazed by a bullet, Kayla saw Rio's car pull up into the lot. A second person was with him, another SVPD officer. Unlike Rio, this officer was in uniform. She watched as Rio angled his long body out of the seat and realized she couldn't be mortally wounded or else she wouldn't be getting aroused as quickly as she was just by looking at Rio. He was at her side in a few short strides. He flashed his badge at the EMT before he put his hand on her upper arm opposite the side where she was injured and looked into her eyes.

"You okay?" His eyes were full of concern, and maybe, just maybe, was that a flash of guilt?

She nodded, but her lower lip started to jerk and without further warning she was blubbering like a baby.

"Can I have a minute with her?" Rio asked but he'd already moved in between her and the first responder.

"Yes, sir, of course."

"I'm, I'm f-f-fine." She hated how out of control she sounded. It was like when she and her brother had just missed being victims of a terrorist bomb on the Tube in London, when they'd been teens. The reality of how close they'd come to being hurt or worse hit her only after she was back at home and her parents' concern had underscored their near miss.

"Yes, you are." Rio's arms were around her and she leaned into his embrace, still sitting on the back end of the ambulance. "You're more than fine, Kayla. I'm so sorry I wasn't here for you."

"How could you have known you needed to be?" She sniffed but didn't miss the way he stiffened at her question.

"I'll tell you about it later." He lifted her chin with his finger. "Did you see anyone?"

She shook her head.

"No. I heard some steps right before the gunshot, but that was it. I was so frightened and didn't see a way out except to try to hide in the hedges. That's what's got me so scratched up—probably more than the bullet." She allowed him to tilt her head and examine her ear. He brushed her hair back just as the EMT had but she felt Rio's touch down into the deepest, scariest parts of herself. His nearness chased away the fear that had terrorized her only minutes before.

"You're right. It's not much more than a scratch. It

looks like he butterflied it up nicely for you, but I'm sure you'll need to have a doctor look at it."

"You're kidding, right? I don't need to go to a doctor. It's stopped bleeding, I don't have a headache or anything and I have a wedding to get planned." Not to mention the other orders waiting for her at the shop. She hadn't even been able to touch base with Jenny yet.

"The wedding planning can wait. Where was Gloria when this happened?" Rio's voice was stern and she heard a steely note of frustration.

"She'd already left, out the front. The only other person meeting with us was Veronique, the chef, and she left as much as a full half hour before we did."

"I need you to come back to the station and file an official report. I promise I'll make it as painless as possible."

"I'll meet you there. I'll take my van this time."

"Kayla, no. If you want to be in your van, let me drive it. I'll have my deputy drive my car back."

Rio listened as Kayla talked to her assistant, Jenny, about the day's workload and what they had in store for tomorrow. As he took the backcountry roads to Silver Valley, he used the opportunity to look at Kayla as much as possible while keeping his driving safe.

Except for the nasty slash across her left ear, she looked like the woman he knew and not the victim of an attempted murder.

Slow down. You don't know they meant to kill her.

Kayla's bleak shock lifted when she spoke with Jenny. Her expression was animated by her enthusiasm for her flower shop and what she loved doing. He liked how she managed to be so personable, but at the same time was definitely the one in charge. It was a skill he'd had to work at, since his inclination as a young officer had been to clean up a mess and ask questions later. Through time, experience and observing that a gentle touch got more answers out of people, he'd learned to do what Kayla seemed to do naturally.

"Any reason you're so interested in my work schedule?" She turned toward him, her annoyance obvious.

"Sorry. I honestly didn't pay attention to what you were saying. I can't keep my eyes off you."

He quickly looked at her and smiled when he saw the blush on her cheeks. Making Kayla speechless was rare and incredibly satisfying.

"Oh."

"You've been thinking about it, too, Kayla. I know you have."

"The stairs." Another thing he adored about Kayla was her straightforward manner when it came to sex. She was as feminine as all get-out yet hadn't hesitated to ask him for what she'd wanted in bed.

"Among other things." He reached over and squeezed her thigh. "Has it occurred to you that we're not done yet, Kayla?"

"It doesn't matter what's occurred to me, Rio. You're still the investigating officer on Keith's case, and we can't get past the fact that we weren't entirely up-front with each other when we got together. You didn't tell me you worked undercover, and I didn't tell you that I wasn't interested in getting involved with someone in your kind of work."

"Maybe." He wasn't willing to tell her about Keith's case being dropped. He'd been on his way to tell Keith when the call came in that she'd been shot at. Keith deserved to know he was free of the wrongful accusations first, and besides, it'd be his business whether he told his sister or not.

"You think it's Gloria, don't you? You think she snuck around back and shot at me." Kayla's tone was rife with the stress of what she'd been through.

"No, I don't think that, not necessarily." Shit. He needed to tell her more. "Look, Kayla, remember, we think there was a second person involved in the murder. There's evidence that someone left the barn out the other side of the building from where you were."

"Then it could have been Gloria, especially if the man I heard was indeed Mickey. It makes sense with them having an affair. But why they'd kill Meredith, together, is what's bothering me."

Rio sighed. "Kayla, you're not on the SVPD. I asked you to keep your eyes and ears open, and I regret that now you've been drawn into it."

"If you're right and if a second person was there, he or she could have doubled back and seen my van, as you said before. They'd both be after me whether or not I agreed to stay on with the wedding." She looked out the windshield but he doubted she saw the rows and rows of neatly planted apple trees on both sides of the road that wound through the orchards like a ribbon. "It's too neat, isn't it? To think that Gloria and Mickey are both murderers. And Gloria seems too, too…" She trailed off and Rio risked a smirk.

"Too high-strung?"

"Exactly. I can't see Gloria handling the stress of a murder conspiracy."

Kayla was getting tired, no doubt the crash after her adrenaline rush catching up to her. "The comedown from a situation as tense as what you've been through today can be a bitch, Kayla. If you need to close your eyes and catch a catnap until I get you home, please do."

"I'm okay. We're stopping at the station first, right?"

"Only for as long as it takes to file your report. Then you're going to get some rest."

He failed to tell her exactly where she was getting some rest. There was no way he'd take her back to her place, not when her name was on a killer's list somewhere.

Chapter 14

It was an Easter Sunday unlike any other Kayla had experienced. She woke up at Rio's and didn't have any last-minute deliveries to take care of. Within a half hour she was with Rio in his car.

"Yes, I'm a little cranky. Wouldn't you be if you'd been shot at yesterday and had to sleep in a strange bed without your own stuff? And to top it off, the Easter Bunny hasn't brought me any chocolates." Kayla pulled her sunglasses out of her tote and put them on as Rio drove the unmarked police vehicle.

"It wasn't a strange bed, not technically." Rio tried to make her smile but she ignored him. "And I'm sorry about your Easter being ruined. Law enforcement works 24/7. You didn't have anything planned with your brother or parents, did you?"

"No, my parents are still out of town and Keith and I were going to wait until they were home to go out for a big brunch. It's too crazy to try to get reservations at Hershey this weekend, anyhow. Thank you, by the way, for keeping your word. I slept so soundly and never worried about a thing all night." She'd wished Rio was there to hold her, but they couldn't afford to go there. Not with this case blowing up around them.

"I'm not going to let anything else happen to you, Kayla." She saw his fingers tighten on the steering wheel.

"You always hold the steering wheel on the bottom. Why?"

He looked surprised.

"Where do you hold it?"

"At ten and two o'clock. Like they taught us in driver's ed."

He smiled. "You're right. I forgot about that. When we go through police training and refresher defensive driving, we're taught to hold it here." He nodded at the four and eight o'clock positions his hands were at. "It gives me more control over the wheel. It's not something that makes too much of a difference until you need to make a quick turn or J-turn."

"I hope I never have to pull any of that crazy stuff in my van."

She watched his jaw tighten and his spine go stiff as he drove. "What, Rio?"

"On the subject of police maneuvers—where we're going is kind of like a police department. But also very different in a lot of ways." He hadn't yet revealed to Kayla where they were headed.

"Oh?"

He remained silent and she sensed he was searching for words.

"Spit it out, Rio. You won't be yourself again until you do. First you tell me to get whatever information I can, then you're angry with me because you think I snooped too much. Now you're looking at me as if you're taking me to prison or something. We're *not* going to the county prison, are we?"

"No, it's not a prison. It's an extra group of law-enforcement folks we work with when we need more help on a case. More often they work their own cases separately from SVPD and use folks like me on an as-needed basis to help with the man hours."

"What does any of this have to do with me?" It didn't surprise her that a man like Rio had his fingers in so many different law-enforcement entities—he was a detective and he'd no doubt had loads of training to do his job.

"You'll see. You have to trust me on this."

Trust Rio.

"The last time I trusted you we ended up naked."

He held up one hand as he kept his focus on the road.

"You slept at my house, and that's all you did. Slept. I know we didn't plan what happened the other night. Maybe it was because of how abruptly we had to break things off. We ended up in bed together so quickly last year, and then Keith's case happened and I had to break it off. I'm sorry about that, Kayla, but you didn't want to pursue a relationship with me, either."

"No, I didn't. I don't. I mean, hell, I don't know what I mean."

His hand was on hers, where it rested on her thigh, and he squeezed. "Let it go for now. We have to focus on keeping you safe. That's why I'm taking you to the headquarters for the Trail Hikers."

"Trail Hikers?"

As succinctly as possible he explained to her the role of the Trail Hikers, how even he didn't know the full extent of their reach despite working with them for several months. That they were a supersecret government shadow agency that had carte blanche to work across all levels of law enforcement to achieve their mission objectives.

"Usually Trail Hikers work on larger, international crimes that have stymied the FBI and CIA. But they also get involved in more local cases, like the True Believers and whatever they are doing in Silver Valley. To be fair, you have to understand that there is often so much more to any one case than I ever know. It's how we keep everyone safe."

"The same way classified information is compartmentalized. My parents worked in embassies and with the military at times. I understand."

She felt his stare and met it. "It's okay, Rio. I'm not going to wilt. I've lived in some pretty rough parts of the world."

"As a child, with your parents and State Department protection. This is different, Kayla. Anything could go wrong at any moment and you might be the only one there to fix it. I can't be there every minute of the day for you."

"As much as you're trying to be." She didn't elicit the dimple she wanted to see in his right cheek. "Come on, Rio, lighten up. We're both still here. And things like this happen all the time. We just happen to be involved in this one."

And she just happened to fear she was falling for Rio again.

He'd watched newbies come into Trail Hikers more than once, but this time was the most personal. Kayla entered the slick professional office building and spoke to the receptionist as a local small business owner, but she'd leave knowing she was going to become part of an elite group of government shadow operatives. While Kayla wouldn't become a full-fledged agent, if she received even a fraction of the training he'd had, it would be enough to change her.

Change was inevitable when you came up against the unrelenting evil that human beings were capable of.

"Kayla, so nice to meet you. I'm Claudia." Claudia shook Kayla's hand before she pointed to the two seats in front of her polished executive desk. "Please, have a seat both of you. Hello, Rio."

"Claudia."

"Kayla, I'm sure Rio has given you a little information about the Trail Hikers and let you know we'd like you to come on board. I'm here to answer any questions you have, and then I'm going to turn you over to

our instructors for three full days of training that will
include weapons handling, starting tomorrow. Are you
okay with this?"

"Yes." Kayla shot Rio a look that let him know to
stay out of it.

"Great. Welcome aboard, and let's get down to some
of the brass tacks of Trail Hikers."

Claudia's informational talk lasted about a half
hour, and although Rio had received the same talk
with Bryce Campbell sitting next to him, he didn't remember a whole lot of it. He'd been too anxious to get
into the training. He wondered if Kayla felt the same.

She constantly surprised him. When he'd fallen for
her last year, he'd been drawn in by her sense of humor
and her intelligence, yes, but mostly by her unstoppa-
ble sexiness. He was willing to admit he'd had shallow
motives in that regard. Yet each time he'd been with
her, she'd shown another facet of herself that made him
realize she wasn't going to be a temporary companion,
not even a friend with benefits.

Kayla was different.

"If you'll sign at the marked spots on these contracts, I'll have our instructor escort you out. Do you
have any questions for me?" Claudia must have said
this spiel to dozens of agents—no one but Claudia
knew the total number of persons involved with the
Trail Hikers—but she looked as enthusiastic and sol-
emn as she had when Rio had signed on.

"No, none at the moment." Kayla signed her name
with a deftness that made it seem she'd always wanted
to become a secret agent.

Rio wanted the True Believers and their criminal ways taken out of town no matter what it took. But as he looked at Kayla's bandaged ear, her scraped-up skin, and thought about how he'd feel if anything irreparable happened to her, doubt at the intelligence of allowing Kayla to get involved so deeply with the case shadowed his vision.

Kayla had never experienced anything like the following three days with the Trail Hikers training team. Luckily it was spring break and Jenny agreed to run the shop. They made their store hours shorter, blaming the upcoming wedding season. It was believable enough as the Charbonneau wedding was indeed consuming most of their hours and budget at the moment.

Since Trail Hikers wasn't going to be a permanent gig for Kayla, they'd given her an abbreviated version of the training. Enough to keep herself safe and help with the case, but not so much that she'd be overwhelmed with needless tactics and information.

After she'd left Rio in Claudia's office, she was taken to the most up-to-date gym she'd ever seen and given workout gear to change into. It was her exact size. She'd had to work around her bruises and ear abrasion, but the movement and self-defense classes were exhilarating when they weren't humbling.

At the end of the third day of her training, Wednesday, Rio was waiting as he had been each of the previous days to take her to his house. True to his word, he'd steered clear of her, allowing her time to rest and watch mindless television in the evenings while he worked on his laptop in the office off the family room.

It was almost as if they were a real couple, except they weren't having sex.

"Ready to conquer the world?" he asked her as she slid onto the leather seat and buckled her belt.

"Not quite. I wish I'd had this training before college, though. There were a few grabby dates I'd have liked to take down a time or two."

His expression froze and she reached to grab his forearm. "Oh, no, Rio, I was never assaulted. I was just trying to be funny. I'm sorry."

"No apology needed." But judging by his unusually gruff tone, she'd overstepped. He was on overdrive with his need to protect her.

"Yes, I do need to apologize. You've done so much for me. Maybe now that I've had some training you can relax a little bit?"

"Never."

"What, don't you trust me with a weapon?"

"You're probably a better shot than I am. That wouldn't surprise me."

As he drove she noticed they weren't taking the usual route to his house. "Where are we going?"

"I thought I'd treat both of us to a nice meal before the shit hits the fan with the wedding."

"You really think it's going to all come to the wedding itself?"

He nodded. "Or the rehearsal dinner. If we're lucky, whoever the second assailant is will be at the Friday function and we'll be able to figure it all out then. That would keep the wedding intact."

"I can't believe Cynthia and Charles are going to go through with it. It's so obviously a political power move."

"The Charbonneau father-daughter duo is destined for political infamy." He entered the expressway and headed south, towards Gettysburg.

"Where is Gloria in all of this?"

"She's the odd one out. Tony picked her because she looked good on his arm."

"I don't think they have the best of relationships, even apart from the affair. I'm surprised she stays with him."

"It's about the money, honey. If he can keep her in the clothes and automobiles she loves, why would she leave him? Especially when she's getting any extra attention she craves from Mickey."

"Mickey. I read the file on him." A good part of her training had been time spent with the files pertaining to Meredith's case that the Trail Hikers had procured. "He's got quite the rap sheet. I'm surprised the mayor risked hiring him in the first place."

"They go way back. They both ran with the same crowd in New Jersey. Once the mayor got elected and Mickey was entrenched in his political staff, Tony knew he couldn't just let him go, not without blowback."

"But why would Mickey get involved with Gloria? He and Cynthia seemed real chummy when I watched them talking in the street to one another."

"Cynthia is her father's daughter. She can charm the pants off anyone, even though she's pretty abrasive when she's trying to get something she wants. Not that I think she wants Mickey's pants off." He grinned.

Kayla groaned. "The thought of that is gross, Rio. Mickey's twice her age."

"Judge Blackwell is even older. Worse, he's a friend of mine and I haven't been able to talk any sense into him about her. He's one of those guys who is so damn smart except when it comes to women."

They remained silent and Kayla noticed how close they were to the Gettysburg battlefield.

"Where on earth are we going? I don't think spending time at the battlefield is going to help relax us."

"We're not going to the battlefield. Have you ever eaten at the Colonial Restaurant?"

"The one with the restaurant in the historical cellar? I love it! Keith and I took our parents there last Thanksgiving."

The mention of Keith's name made Rio stiffen. He knew Kayla saw his reaction. It was time to come clean.

"Kayla, about Keith…"

"I know, Rio."

"You know what?" Always full of surprises, this woman.

"Keith is the person I was talking to on the phone last night when you walked into the bedroom to get your clothes." She'd been in bed, Rio's bed, with her e-reader and about to fall asleep when Keith called. "I can't thank you enough for all you've done. He told me he'd be back at work today, with all charges dropped and nothing on his record."

"I didn't do anything but my job."

"Don't lie to me. You didn't have to go meet with the Sneads, but you did." He looked at her, surprised that she knew the name of the couple. "I read the files. Claudia told me to read anything that had to do with Silver Valley and the True Believers, in case I stumble upon a connection during the wedding. Also to help me find the other suspect, if we're sure there's one."

"Back to Mickey Ippolito. I think his affair with Gloria is a way to keep her in his control. So that she doesn't screw over Tony, pardon the pun. A woman like Gloria can be dangerous when she's not getting the attention she craves."

"I guess that makes sense."

"I think so. Now, has anything triggered a memory of the murder night for you?"

"Don't change the subject, Rio. We were talking about how wonderful a detective and public servant you are. Why didn't you tell me you'd talked to the Sneads?"

"It wasn't my story to tell. Keith deserved to tell you first."

And he had. Her older brother's voice had been as filled with gratitude for what Rio had accomplished as it was with excitement at returning to work.

"That was nice of you. To let Keith tell me first."

"I aim to please. Sometimes." They both laughed. He pulled into the front parking lot of the restaurant. It was housed in a beautiful building built before the Revolutionary War. "They're busy tonight." Rio drove through the packed lot until they found a spot behind the restaurant. When he opened her door, Kayla stood up and felt the muscles in her legs and shoulders twinge.

"You didn't tell me I'd be getting the workout of my life the last few days." She stretched to one side, then the other.

"Sore, are you?" He stepped behind her and before she realized what he was doing he started kneading her shoulders with just the right amount of pressure.

"We're in broad daylight, Rio." Still, a moan of pleasure worked past her lips. His fingers were magic.

"I'm massaging your shoulders, that's all. Unless you want more?"

"Stop teasing. We have an agreement."

"We did. Before. And I don't remember putting anything in writing." But he stopped. She turned to face him. A cool spring breeze made what could have been a warm night chilly and she wrapped her large scarf more tightly around her.

"We still do, right? We're in the middle of the biggest thing I've ever faced. And it's not just about us anymore, is it?" She searched his face, his eyes. In the dimming light she saw the desire in his eyes, but his serious expression told her that he was every bit as focused as she was on finding the murderer.

"No, it isn't."

He touched her forehead with his and wrapped his arms loosely around her waist. "I wish it was simpler, babe." The way he said the word *babe* made her want to insist they get back in the car and go home. To his place, to make love all night.

Now that she was a Trail Hiker, no matter how temporary her position with the agency, she had an obligation to the greater good. To her home and Rio's.

"The events of the past week make being upset at you for being a cop seem so petty."

"All things are relative."

"You didn't lie, not outright."

He chuckled. "No, but I didn't tell you everything, either. That was my first mistake."

"There were more?"

"I'm not going to talk about that tonight. Let's go in and have a nice meal. Take a break from all of the work that awaits us over the next few days." He brushed her lips with his, lightly, sweetly.

It touched her more deeply than the intensely passionate kisses they'd shared while making love.

The tinkling spring ran next to their table and Kayla looked at her dinner companion in the dim light. Candles were all that lit the dining room, which consisted of several booths and tables placed closely together in the former colonial family cellar.

"I love coming here and imagining how the first owners lived here. These walls lived through the American Revolution."

"I agree. I'm a pretty big colonial history buff."

"Me, too. Who's your favorite historical figure?"

"Benjamin Franklin. Yours?"

"Same. Although I've been reading quite a bit lately

about the women who played key roles during the revolution. We always get left out of the history books."

"Do you fancy yourself as a colonial spy?"

"Funny you should ask. In high school we were living in the Netherlands and I was attending an international school. I did a report on the revolution and included facts about how the Americans used espionage and guerrilla warfare, much to the dismay of the British."

"American innovation. We still have it."

"Do we ever. If I had ever doubted that, being read into TH would certainly have changed my mind..." She drifted and took a long sip of her ale. They'd picked a beer on tap that they both enjoyed instead of sharing a bottle of wine. She couldn't handle more than one drink after such long, exhausting training, and Rio was driving.

"Listen, Kayla. I know things are still crazy right now. But we need to talk more. About us." His tone had changed and the flutters in her stomach told her so had his intent. He put down his beer and reached over for her hands. "I don't want you to get the wrong idea from me. I'm staying away, keeping my distance, because you need the time and energy to devote to what you've just learned. It's a lot to absorb, going from full-time florist to part-time undercover agent. Who is facing a lot of dangerous situations during this investigation, by the way."

"Well, I've been trained now, at least in some basic tactics and evasions. So hopefully, there won't be any more close calls."

"It's not so simple, Kayla. Training and feeling confident in the instructional scenarios is quite different from when it happens in real life."

"Don't you think I already know that? This is very real to me, Rio. I saw Meredith get shot. I was in the next room while the mayor's wife was scheming with her lover. I just wish I'd had the training then…"

He squeezed her hands. "You didn't, and you did fine. If you'd had the training, you might have tried to take down a dangerous man."

"Maybe I would have gotten him, though—and then no one else would be in danger."

Rio didn't have the heart to tell Kayla that her chances of catching and apprehending the suspect without getting badly hurt—or worse—were slim to none.

"You may be right." Her hands were so soft and the easy way she accepted his affection made it difficult to keep his promise to himself, and to her, to put their relationship on hold until after the case was wrapped up.

"I know I'm just a part-time helper, in the big picture of law enforcement, and what I've just learned is basically how to keep myself safe while not getting in the way of the professionals. Like you." She gave him an impish smile and he reflexively smiled back. "Still, it feels good to be part of the team and not just flat-out prey to whoever we're dealing with."

"I've been amazed by your bravery this entire time." He brushed the side of her cheek with his fingertips and then released her hands completely, leaning back as the waitress delivered their food.

"Oh, my goodness, I had no idea how I hungry I was until I smelled this." She dug into her crock of French onion soup, pulling up a long strand of melted mozzarella. "It doesn't get any better than this."

As he watched her enjoyment, he had to agree.

Chapter 15

"Is there any way to figure out how the cult is connected to the charges against Mayor Donner, like you did with Keith Paruso?" Colt Todd ate a doughnut while discussing the role of the True Believers in Silver Valley's political doings. Rio found it odd that his boss was giving in to his sweet tooth a day earlier than usual. Usually the superintendent only indulged on Fridays.

"No, her case is much more complicated. And even if I could prove that the charges against her were fabricated, it's up to the judge now."

"Judge Blackwell." Colt finished his doughnut and looked at Rio, a frown at odds with the delicious maple-glazed confection he'd just enjoyed. "Who is marrying into the Charbonneau clan."

"I wouldn't give them the credit of being a clan. More like a gang." Rio didn't hide his disgust for the politically driven family. "So. We have a mayor with a trophy wife. A wife who is having an affair with the mayor's assistant, who appears to be playing both sides in this. He wants to keep Gloria distracted, so she doesn't catch on to any of Tony's illegal activities and possibly blackmail him. Meanwhile, the mayor's daughter is a ball-buster who thinks she's already running the state, not to mention Silver Valley."

"You figured this all out in the past few days?"

"With the help of Kayla's information, yes."

Colt bunched up his napkin and tossed it easily into the wastebasket across his office. "Two points." He nodded at Rio. "I know you don't want her involved in this at all, except from a purely observational standpoint. I'm in agreement with Claudia on this, however. We don't have the manpower or the luxury of planning time to get enough agents undercover at the wedding this weekend. We need her."

"Speaking of planning, do we have a name for our op against the True Believers yet? We're certain they're here, and with the fallout from the Female Preacher Killer case and the fact that the lawyer working against Keith Paruso is a former cult member, it's clear we need to bring them down."

"We're still in the prevention stage here, Rio. Once I name an op against members of a former cult that existed in upstate New York, it becomes interstate. The big guns will be here quicker than I ate that doughnut."

"We already have the big guns, though." Rio referred to the Trail Hikers, who were keeping tight tabs on the convicted cult members as they were released from prison in New York and sought probation in Pennsylvania. So far each and every former member had made their way into Silver Valley and taken up residence in the same trailer park.

"Right. And I'd like to keep it with the Trail Hikers for now. We're lucky they've taken an interest in the cult and what it's up to. It eases some of our workload, and the pain in the ass it's going to be when the Feds need our work spaces."

"Roger that, boss."

Rio knew Colt never begrudged any work done with or for the FBI, Treasury Department, Homeland Security or other federal law enforcement. SVPD was a small operation compared to what was needed to take down a ring of cultists or crime syndicates and the last time they'd had help from federal entities, the SVPD police station had been shoulder to shoulder with officers and agents for almost a month straight.

"Your job is to find out who murdered Meredith Houseman and who took a shot at Kayla."

"I'm headed over to the flower shop now."

Colt held up his hand. "Hang on a minute, Rio." Rio didn't like where he thought this was going.

"You think it's your job to protect Kayla, and whatever your personal relationship with her was or is, she's been trained by the best in how to keep herself out of trouble. I know she hasn't had the full-on training, but the Trail Hikers can do more in three days than other agencies do in three months. You don't need to hover

over her. She'll take care of herself. Your time needs to go into finding the killer. Am I clear?"

"Yes, sir." Damn it, he didn't disagree with his boss, but it still stung to be called out like an adolescent with his first crush.

"Have Kayla keep a low profile, collecting whatever info she can, and with any luck we'll catch a killer by the wedding on Saturday."

Colt stood up, indicating their meeting was finished. Rio stood, too, and nodded. "Yes, sir."

"And, Rio?"

"Yes, sir?"

"Remember to keep yourself out of trouble, too."

Kayla spent all of Thursday and most of Friday morning prepping for the weekend's deliveries, leaving the rest of Friday and all of Saturday free to entirely focus on the rehearsal dinner and wedding.

"Are you sure you're okay with handling the deliveries and the new orders? Plus showing up early on Saturday to help with the wedding?" she asked Jenny. Kayla had amended her shop hours to facilitate the wedding's demands.

Jenny nodded with youthful enthusiasm. "I've got it. All my exams are essays or reports this semester, so it's a lot easier for my time management." Kayla looked at Jenny's day planner, which had more Post-its and Japanese highlighter tape than blank space. "You are an expert at that. I could use some of your techniques."

"You're kidding, right? I don't know how you manage this shop, keep the orders straight, make new arrangements and decorating ideas up, and handle the customers. Plus deliveries. Crazy!"

Kayla laughed at Jenny's outburst. "It's all part of the business. You could do it, too. At least all the chaos has finally convinced me to hire a delivery person and maybe another assistant."

"Any idea when they'll start?" Jenny looked so hopeful.

"Sorry, it won't be until after this wedding is over." And her first op with the Trail Hikers was finished. It would probably be her *only* op, but a small part of her hoped that all the work she'd done wasn't for nothing.

"If you need any suggestions on who to hire, let me know. The delivery job would be perfect for some of my school friends."

"I will. I'm sure we won't have any trouble finding someone to do it. It's the timing that's critical. I'll want the deliveries out and done before noon each day whenever possible. You and I can pick up the stragglers in the afternoons."

"Sounds good. Do you mind if I leave now?" Jenny had asked earlier if she could take off early in light of the long hours she'd be putting in for the wedding. By tomorrow all they needed to do was get to the inn and set up the table arrangements for the reception, well ahead of the wedding party, which would need a couple of hours for official photographs. They'd have the flowers for the gazebo and the mayor's home done by early tomorrow morning, as long as the weather held.

"No, go ahead. I've got the rehearsal dinner covered for tonight. Thanks again for all you've done, Jenny."

"Do you want me to turn off the open sign? I know you still have a lot of paperwork to get done."

"That's okay, leave the door open. I'll handle whoever might come in."

As Jenny left, Kayla ignored the thought she couldn't seem to shake. That she hoped Rio would stop by. They'd agreed that she'd stay at his place until the murderer was apprehended. Before she'd signed on to the Trail Hikers, she would have thought it was a crazy idea, but after learning about the vast resources they had, combined with her faith in Rio and SVPD, she was confident they'd catch the killer soon.

And then she'd go back to living alone.

The shop door chimed as a familiar figure walked in. At first Kayla couldn't place the young woman, but then she realized why she knew her.

Meredith's sister. She'd come in with her family after the murder to order flowers for Meredith's funeral. The funeral had only been yesterday, as the body had to be released from the coroner before the family held the service.

"Can I help you?"

"Yes, I'm Mica. Mica Houseman?"

"Hello, Mica. I remember you, of course. How are you holding up? How are your parents?"

Tears welled in the girl's eyes and Kayla walked around the counter to put a comforting arm around her. "I'm so sorry, Mica. I know this is an awful time for you and your family."

Mica nodded, then wiped her tears.

"Yes, yes, it is. That's why I'm here."

How sweet. Here she was suffering and grieving, but wanted to get flowers for someone else. "What can I do for you, Mica?"

"I saw you with Detective Ortega." Kayla froze. What did she mean?

"Oh?"

Mica sniffed. "I work at the Colonial Restaurant, in the gift shop. I saw you go in with him on Wednesday. I kept working my shifts until Meredith's funeral. I had to stay busy." She paused a long moment as if gathering courage. "Are you close? With Detective Ortega?"

Kayla wasn't sure where this was going, but she felt she owed Meredith's sister the truth.

"We were. We're friends now."

"You looked like a lot more than friends." Kayla wished circumstances were different and that Mica's observation was accurate, but she wasn't going to try to explain the complicated bond she and Rio shared.

"We've known one another...awhile."

"I'm only asking because I need to be able to trust that you can get him a message from me."

Kayla's instincts kicked in at the same time as her Trail Hikers training. *Keep her talking.* She stood back and looked at Mica directly. "Of course you can. We talk daily, and I can reach him at any moment. Would you feel more comfortable if he was here?"

"No!" Mica's vehement reply belied the shaking woman who'd been weeping minutes earlier. "I can't talk to him or see him. It's too dangerous for my family. I can't put them at risk, not after what happened to Meredith. But he needs to know."

"Know what?"

"Do you have a catalogue or portfolio of your services?"

"Of course." Kayla took a pamphlet from the acrylic holder on the counter and handed it to her.

"I'm acting like I'm reading this and picking out an arrangement in case anyone is watching me. I'm placing the flash drive that Meredith gave me a copy of two weeks ago into this. She told me not to ask questions and not to look at it. She said she needed a safe place to keep her file backup. After she died, I looked at it. I was afraid to tell anyone because I don't want to put anyone else in my family in danger. I didn't know if I could trust the police, since this was the mayor's assistant. They're always showing corruption on the news, you know. I knew this flash drive, what's on it, was important to Meredith, but I had no idea it was something that could, could…get her killed." She faltered and a tear fell onto the pamphlet Mica was pretending to read.

"It's okay, Mica. No one's coming in here and you're safe. As a matter of fact, it's time to close the shop." Kayla went and locked the front door and turned off the open sign, then flipped off the overhead lighting. "Let's go into the back area to talk, where no one can see us from the street."

For the first time in her life, Kayla was carrying a weapon and couldn't imagine how vulnerable she'd feel if she didn't have a way to protect her and Mica in this moment. Because she had no doubt that Mica had whatever had given the killer motive to murder Meredith.

* * *

"Meredith was über-organized. When we were little, her side of the bedroom was always color-coded and her bed looked as though it had been made by a hotel maid. I was the messy one, with my dolls all over the place." Mica's eyes brightened at the happy memory and Kayla's heart squeezed for the pain she was in.

"You said when she gave you this flash drive she didn't say anything about what was on it?"

Mica shook her head. "No. I'm not sure she knew it was as dangerous as it obviously is. Of course, when I looked at it I immediately knew that someone else out there is aware of the numbers, of what it means."

Indeed. They sat in the workshop, and Kayla had made sure the back door was locked and bolted before booting up her laptop, where she and Mica perused the spreadsheets and summary documents Meredith had saved to the drive.

"This isn't just about the mayoral election being rigged. It's clear the votes were fraudulent—look how many of the people who voted don't actually reside in Silver Valley."

"So they got fake IDs?" Kayla was stymied as statistics and political science weren't her favorite subjects in college.

"Either that or when different locals voted, the votes registered more than once. And look at this." Mica opened a text document titled Truth. Kayla quickly read it.

"Meredith's saying that someone hacked into the

voting system and allowed a substantial number of fake votes for Charbonneau."

"Yes."

"So it's what we thought. The election was rigged. And the mayor is getting ready to pass some shady legislation that will be advantageous to the big businesses in town that support him, while crippling the little guys who don't jump on his bandwagon."

"That's what I see. But I'm a physical-education teacher, not an accountant or systems expert. I have no idea how these things actually happen."

Kayla didn't, either, but knew who would. "I don't understand why Meredith didn't go directly to the authorities."

Mica snorted. "The entire staff, if not the town and county seats, are corrupt. There's at least one bad apple in each, if not more. Meredith knew she'd be run out of her job and ridiculed if she reported it too hastily, to the wrong person. She said that since Mayor Donner had been kicked out it was awful working for Silver Valley. No one knew who to trust. The new mayor kept Meredith as a sign of good faith, that she would provide continuity between the two administrations. When she realized what was really happening, though…" Mica sniffed, wiping her eyes. "She was going to call a friend in the FBI the next week. Before…"

"We're going to make sure that whoever's responsible for her death is caught, Mica." At Mica's puzzled expression, Kayla covered her tracks. "I mean SVPD and Detective Ortega. I'll get this to him. If it's the new mayor, he's as good as caught."

"I can't believe such scum can get away with something like this. That they even think they can."

"Even the mayor of an average town in America can let power go to his head."

"Maybe he's compensating for something..." Mica said, even as distraught as she was.

Kayla laughed. "You've got that right. Let me get this to Rio, Detective Ortega, and I'll let you know what happens."

"I don't need to know how it happens, Kayla. I only need to know that he gets it and that they catch the bastard who murdered my sister."

"Meredith had the goods on him, all right." Claudia's voice was quiet behind Rio and Kayla as they all huddled around a computer screen at Trail Hikers headquarters. After Kayla had called Rio about Mica's visit, he'd told her to meet him at the TH headquarters with the flash drive.

"Are you going to arrest him tonight?" Kayla wished she could be there to see Tony Charbonneau's usually overconfident smug expression change to horror when he realized the jig was up.

"No. We have this evidence, and it definitely incriminates the mayor and most likely his assistant, Mickey, in electoral fraud and a bucket load of other charges, but we still can't tie them directly to the murder." Rio's reasonable tone indicated this wasn't his first rodeo.

"Rio's correct. We have to get the killers, and hard evidence on them."

"But the longer we wait, the better chance that the

mayor will know someone else has the goods on him. Don't you worry about him taking off, disappearing overseas or something? And we know the mayor is at *least* peripherally involved. And then there's Gloria. She's in this somehow."

"If we were certain he has a large sum of money stashed offshore, sure. But he doesn't as far as we know, and his type is in it for the power and glory. He'll never give up his office without a huge fight." Claudia spoke with certainty. "I've seen this time and again with political criminals. Mostly during my time in the military, granted. But military or civilian, it makes no difference when it comes to the bad guys who are power hungry. What slips them up is their greed. It looks like our mayor got too greedy after winning the election. Now he thinks he's going to push through ugly legislation that could turn Silver Valley into a haven for people like him—sleazy, power-hungry criminals."

"Gloria's nothing more than an opportunist." Rio's voice was as assured as Claudia's. "She married Charbonneau because she perceived him as the powerful, rich man she needed to take her places."

"Agreed. Trail Hikers did a thorough background check on her and she's from a seedy neighborhood in northern New Jersey. Her mother left her when she was very young, and her father had a string of women throughout her life. She moved out when she was seventeen, working as a shampoo girl in a strip mall. Gloria earned her cosmetology degree and met Tony when he regularly came into the barbershop she was working in. He was still legally married to Cynthia's mother when they began their relationship. He'd never bothered to file for divorce when she took off years earlier. She was a drug addict with mental illness."

"How do you get all of this information?" Kayla asked it as a question but it was more of an afterthought. "I thought it took ages to get this kind of detailed data."

Claudia's expression remained neutral. "It's one of the advantages of being a government shadow agency. We have connections to intelligence that SVPD, with all due respect, doesn't."

"One of the many reasons I'm grateful for Trail Hikers. I wasn't its biggest fan in the beginning but if it helps us bring these bastards to justice any sooner, saves one more life, it's worth the extra effort having a second job takes." Rio kept scrolling through the spreadsheet and Kayla had no doubt that he was absorbing every detail. Rio's ability to multitask astounded Kayla, and while she felt comfortable creating an intricate floral arrangement while taking an order for a prom wristlet and watching the shop's front door for new customers, her daily tasks didn't involve saving lives.

"Why don't we turn these files over to our data analysts for now? You both have work to do and our time is dwindling."

"What, exactly, am I supposed to do at the rehearsal dinner and wedding, besides observe?"

Claudia motioned to the seats in front of her desk. "Keep talking, and listening." She pressed a button somewhere on her computer and within two heartbeats her receptionist was in the office with them. "Take this to IA and tell them I need a full summary of their findings ASAP. This op has priority."

"Sure thing, Claudia." The young woman disappeared through the thick, soundproof door. Kayla knew that IA was Information Analysis, the busiest department in Trail Hikers. There were analysts trained in varying levels of cybersecurity, intelligence and data analysis, along with dedicated database experts. Rio had mentioned that if SVPD had an iota of the power that existed in the Trail Hikers IA department, there'd be little chance of any criminal ever escaping justice in Silver Valley—or all of Central Pennsylvania for that matter.

"Kayla, we brought you in here because we trust you, and you have the perfect background to handle the kind of cases the Trail Hikers take on, due to your upbringing overseas. We ran background checks on you because of your proximity to the Female Preacher Killer case, so we know you're able to hold a clearance. Since you've found yourself in the middle of the murder of the mayor's assistant, it's useful to us that you can stay close to the family in your role as a florist. We believe that both the FPK case and this murder are connected, whether directly or more tangentially, to the infiltration of Silver Valley by the former members of the True Believers. The FPK wasn't tied to the cult, but the churchgoers who tried to bring charges against your brother were represented by a former cult member. Although thanks to Rio's concentrated efforts, that's history now."

"You really believe they're trying to set up in Silver Valley, don't you?"

"It's not what I believe that's the issue, Kayla. It's the evidence and facts that tell the story. Rio, what's your take after looking at a bit of the data?"

"It looks like simple accounting data. Until IA gets into it, I can't be certain, but I'm thinking they're going to discover that the new mayor and a few of his closest confidants have not only been elected illegally, but that former Mayor Donner was kicked out of office on false charges. It will tie back to the True Believers, just like the case against Keith and the SV Fire Department did, though I don't know how yet. We have to work from what we know of how they operate. The True Believers make it easy for themselves. They don't try to brainwash someone like you—" he looked at Kayla and Claudia "—or me, but rather, they exploit the weak. Those already on the fringes of participating in regular, everyday society as we understand it.

"In the case of the Charbonneaus, they're too strong to ever believe the evil nonsense someone like Leonard Wise preaches. But they are power-greedy and liable to fall for a chance to start a legitimate political career. They wouldn't hesitate to take funds from them and use their help to get Tony elected. Of course, now Tony owes them."

"How did they get residency and set their sights on Silver Valley? Why not another town in the state or back in New Jersey?" Kayla wished they'd never come to Silver Valley.

"We don't know all of those answers yet, Kayla, but

you and Rio may find them out in due course. What I need you to do is keep listening, keep observing and stay alive. I'd like you wired for the wedding. Rio will handle it. The rehearsal dinner will be too scattered and the venue too noisy, but you may capture some significant conversations while you're placing the flowers at the house." Claudia's face bore no evidence of the long hours this was forcing all of them to put in and Kayla silently wondered how the woman managed to do it. "Where will I get wired? Here or at SVPD?"

"Here, or even better, at my place. If you're seen going to and from SVPD by anyone, it will definitely put the Charbonneaus on the defensive." Rio put his hand on her forearm. "Which could get you killed."

Kayla didn't miss that Claudia noted the personal gesture, but unlike a place such as SVPD, or even her floral shop, it didn't seem out of place in Claudia's office. It was as if the CEO of the secret agency trusted her agents no matter how part-time Kayla was to the agency.

"I've got the world's best training, remember? I understand that it's preliminary, though, and that I'm not a full-blown agent. I won't take any unnecessary risks. I'm not going to get killed and we're going to take these losers down." She never thought she'd ever say those kinds of words about a wedding, but so be it. Her childhood had taught her to be adaptable in many difficult situations, and her recent training empowered her to continue in the same manner. And if worse came to worst, Kayla had the small pistol she'd wear at both events this weekend.

Chapter 16

"I'd say it's been a successful night." Kayla was next to Gloria, who stood apart from the crowd at the Serenity Inn's bar. They had moved from the dining room after dinner was cleared.

"Yes. Thank you again for finding those gavels. Charles was touched. Did you see him smile?"

She hadn't, but wanted to keep Gloria talking. "Yes, he's so happy to be marrying Cynthia." She thought he was getting screwed, since Cynthia was all about Cynthia, but it wasn't her concern. "And it's so nice to see how his children have all accepted her so warmly."

Gloria snickered. "Don't let it fool you. Those kids are all on the fast track to stellar law careers like their father. They don't like Cynthia but they don't want to upset their father, and the source of their security." Gloria's face was twisted into a shrewish expression.

"They seem friendly enough to me." The judge's children were adults, with the youngest graduating from Dickinson College with a political science degree. Coincidentally, Cynthia attended law school there. Did Cynthia spend time with Blackwell's youngest or any of the other two kids? She didn't see it, unless it helped Cynthia get closer to their father.

Cynthia looked over her shoulder from a rotating stool at the bar and spied Kayla speaking to Gloria. Within seconds she was with them, her makeup still perfect and her low-cut black cocktail dress highlighting the perfectly round shape of what Kayla assumed were C or D cups. Like the rest of her, they'd probably been bought.

"What are you still doing here, Kayla? We don't need any more flowers tonight, that's for sure." Cynthia took a swig from a drink that looked like a gin and tonic with a lime garnish, but she certainly wasn't acting intoxicated.

"I was checking in to see if you need anything else tonight. If not, I'll see you in the morning. I'll be at the house by eight to check on the work Jenny did tonight."

"Don't wake us up if we're still sleeping." Cynthia took another sip. Gloria looked uncomfortable, as if she'd rather be anywhere else but next to her stepdaughter.

"Regardless of when you get there, please feel free to come into the house in the morning. I'm having a breakfast and brunch catered up until thirty minutes before the ceremony. Help yourself to a meal and, of course, coffee."

"Thank you, I appreciate that." She had no intention of having a cozy brunch with the Charbonneaus, but she might be able to use the excuse to do additional investigative work inside their home.

"If you'll excuse me, I need to go," Cynthia said, giving Kayla a pointed stare as if to say *You need to go, too.* Kayla wasn't sure what bothered Cynthia about her, but something obviously did, right from their first meeting at the mayor's house. Kayla walked back toward the bar.

"It's not you, you know. She's mean to everyone she works with and even her closest friends." Gloria spoke as if she'd recited the words several times.

"I'm sure it's just wedding jitters." Kayla wasn't sure of that at all, but wasn't about to express her real thoughts. "I'll collect the centerpieces and deliver them in the morning if you'd like."

"Oh, no, I only want what we've planned for tomorrow at the house. I don't care what happens to these."

"Okay, then, see you in the morning." Kayla had hoped to use cleaning up the flower arrangements as another way to extend her time at the rehearsal dinner. At least she could ask Molly if it was okay to leave the flowers on the tables. As she walked past the bar toward the kitchen's swinging doors, she took note of who was still at the function. Charles Blackwell was at one corner of the bar with a few men and their wives, all about the same age. She'd seen his children depart right after the cake had been cut. Cynthia held court with her bridal attendants, who were mostly her age and from New Jersey. Gloria stood next to Tony, at the end of the bar with Mickey, Sylvia and a few other people Kayla figured were extended family members.

Molly was in the midst of cleanup in the kitchen, looking frazzled. She smoothed out her expression when she saw Kayla approach. "What can I do for you?"

"Nothing, I just need to know if you can use the flower arrangements. They don't want them and I'd hate to see them go to waste."

"Yes, we can definitely use them for a catered tea tomorrow. It's a ninetieth birthday celebration and since the local assisted-living facility is throwing it, they're on a tight budget."

"Wonderful. Do you need me to move them to another room?"

"You don't have to. One of the busboys can do it in the morning."

"No, really, I'd like to. You've been so nice to work with, as always." Kayla was thrilled that she'd garnered more time on site. At least this way she'd be obviously doing a real job instead of loitering.

"Well, then, okay. If you place them on the banquet table in the other room, we'll get them on the tables in the morning after we put the linens down. Good luck with the wedding tomorrow. They're an interesting family to work for, aren't they?"

"Very much so. Anything crazy happen while you've been here?"

She nodded. "Crazy is the theme for this entire

event. It was such short notice, which is fine, but then Mrs. Charbonneau kept calling with different requests for food and table placement. For a rehearsal dinner! I can't imagine how nuts it'll be tomorrow."

"So you dealt mostly with Gloria?"

"No, not entirely. Cynthia was here a few times, and one thing she asked that no one else ever did was how late we're all used to staying after an event. She was concerned that the party would go too late. I guess she's worried about people being hungover at the wedding tomorrow."

"It doesn't look to me like anyone's over-imbibing."

"No, but if they stay here another hour, they definitely might. They'll probably be on their way soon enough, though."

"True. Thanks again for your support, Molly. I'll get the flowers moved." Kayla left the kitchen and noticed the people at the bar had left. Only the mayor, Cynthia and Charles remained. She wondered where Gloria was, but simply made a beeline for the first two flower arrangements, not wanting to draw attention.

She lifted one heavy arrangement in each hand. Once in the dimly lit corridor between the event rooms, she took care to keep from spilling the water out of the shallow dishes.

The other room was equally dim and she set the arrangements on the long rectangular table nearest the door. As she turned to leave, she heard murmurs and froze. They weren't the overspill of voices from the bar. Someone was in the room.

She turned around and surveyed each corner of the

room. Empty. But off to the left, beyond the buffet table, was an alcove that she remembered led into the kitchen a different way. Since there was no event in this room, no one was using that entrance to the kitchen.

Almost on tiptoe, she walked closer, straining to hear voices.

"You haven't looked at me once all night."

Gloria. And it had to be Mickey with her. Kayla squatted and got underneath the full-length tablecloth. Under the table and behind the linen, she was virtually invisible to anyone who came in and out of the room. Crawling as close to the end of the table as possible, she sat still and forced her breathing to be quiet.

"It's not the time for us to be doing anything, Gloria. We can't take a chance now. There are too many eyes around."

"What are you worried about? Tony's not going to be charged with the murder, and you didn't have anything to do with it. Right, Mickey? You weren't lying to me, were you?"

"No, I would never lie to you." Silence and then smacking noises. Kayla had to work on not making a disgusted noise. Quite the demonstrative "secret" couple, they were.

"Oh, Mickey, I just want to have our regular schedule back. It's been hell with the wedding."

"It'll all be over tomorrow, don't worry. After that we'll get back to what we both like best." More stomach-churning noises of Gloria and Mickey's kisses floated to Kayla. She wondered if she should get out from under the table while she could, when no one would see her here. She didn't want to get stuck and risk someone seeing her crawl out from under the structure.

As the sounds became more intense, she made her move to escape. Getting out from under the table was easy enough, and she had her hand up to push open the door to the small hallway when it opened and Cynthia came barreling into the room. They collided with one another and Kayla's first thought was to reach for her weapon, which was securely strapped to her thigh. But Kayla didn't want Cynthia to know about the gun, and as they stepped back from each other, Kayla realized she needn't worry. Cynthia had a distracted look on her face.

"What are you still doing here?" Flashing eyes and a furrowed brow reflected her ire.

"I'm moving the flower arrangements for the inn. Then I'll be on my way." Kayla was very aware of Gloria and Mickey in the alcove. Did Cynthia know they were there, too?

"I'm looking for my father. Have you seen him?"

"At the bar with you, a couple of minutes ago. Maybe he's in the restroom?" Cynthia acted as if she didn't hear her as she looked around the room.

"I don't think so."

"Maybe he went out for some air. It was getting a little overheated in the bar."

Cynthia assessed her and Kayla saw a vision of the attorney she'd be in a short time. Hard. Intense. Unforgiving. Then the usual mask of supreme perfection was back and Cynthia nodded. "You're right. He's probably in his car, waiting for Gloria."

"She might be with him." Kayla looked to see if Cynthia's expression changed, but the girl was made of granite. "Maybe. I'll go check." Cynthia turned and left the room. Kayla followed but headed past the bar and into the larger event room instead of the exit.

She thought of shouting a "you're welcome" over her shoulder to Gloria and Mickey. She'd just saved them a nasty moment with Cynthia.

When she took the remaining arrangements into the room, there were no more murmurs, and she purposefully placed the flowers at the end of the table, where she was in full view of anyone in the alcove. It was empty. Gloria and Mickey had left in the short time since she and Cynthia had been here.

By the time she'd finished ten minutes later, only Cynthia and Mickey were at the bar. Charles had called it a night, she'd heard Cynthia telling him that she'd call him when she got in and for him to go on home "for your last night as a bachelor." Kayla didn't think a grieving widower truly classified as a bachelor and wondered if Charles would even have looked twice at Cynthia had he been in a clearer emotional state.

Mickey and Cynthia seemed to be enjoying a last nightcap together as she walked out, with no sign of the mayor and his wife. She hoped she didn't have to hear or see any more of Gloria and Mickey in the throes of their forbidden lust.

She shook her head to herself as she headed out to her van. Those two were going to get caught sooner or later, and it wasn't going to be pretty. Uncovering an affair between Gloria and Mickey had simply been collateral information gleaned during this case, however. She still had her sights on finding out who had killed Meredith Houseman and who had tried to kill her.

A dark figure stood next to her van and she paused, reflexively reaching under her skirt for her weapon.

"Relax, it's me." Rio emerged to stand under the parking-lot light, his hand light on her arm. "You okay?"

"I was fine until you just scared me half to death. But I'm good, really. How long have you been here?"

She saw a flash of white as he smiled. "Since dark. We have a couple of plainclothesmen in the restaurant and they let me know when dinner was almost over. I caught a ride with the car that's taking them back to SVPD headquarters."

"If I'd known you were here I could have left sooner."

"No, you couldn't. Let's talk in the van."

She drove while Rio took notes on her observations. It was intimate in the darkness as they talked. Whenever she was near him, she was hyperaware of her surroundings. It was her defense mechanism to keep from thinking about what they'd done on her stairs, what she wanted to do again with him.

"Hiding under that table was smart, but I hate to think of how long you could have been stuck there if you didn't get out when you did."

"Or what else I would have heard. Yuck." She glanced over at him for a brief moment. "I had already decided I'd pretend I'd lost an earring and was looking under the table for it."

"And you would have gotten away with it. Me, I don't have any piercings."

"You never would have fit under the table. You're too big." Desire settled between her legs as she verbalized what she'd fought to keep her mind off the entire time she'd been staying with Rio. Him. His body. Their bodies together.

"You're doing an incredible job, Kayla." The rough edge to his voice made her flush, and when he started to knead her neck with his fingers, she had to work to stay focused on the road. "Rio, don't. We've done well so far."

"Except for the stairs."

She blew out a breath. "Yeah, well, we're only human. It's been very unsettling this past week or so, for sure. It's not like I ever thought I'd be involved with a murder case."

"You're a strong woman. It's why you're so independent." His right hand massaged her neck as she drove and she didn't complain. She was getting tired of fighting her attraction to Rio.

It's not just the attraction. You care about him.

She'd never stopped caring about him.

"Have you reconsidered your vow to stay single for as long as possible?" His voice wasn't mocking or cajoling. Honest and filled with hope, perhaps?

"I'll admit that after seeing the shenanigans between Gloria and Mickey, I should be more skeptical of marriage and happily-ever-after. And to see Cynthia wrap Charles in her Machiavellian web is frightening. It's highlighted for me that maybe it's okay to make a lifetime commitment—but only if it's the right person and not one minute sooner." She'd never spoken words like this before but they didn't surprise her. It was a thought that had been rolling around in her head a lot, more since she and Rio had been forced to be together each day.

"You're scaring me, Kayla. You sound like you've talked yourself out of one of the reasons we broke up."

"There was nothing to break up. We were barely dating."

"We were more than friends with benefits. We *are* more than that, and now you're finally admitting it." Rio's conviction rattled her to her toes. It wasn't what scared her, though. What frightened her was that she wasn't afraid.

Being with Rio day in and day out felt natural. Normal. Right.

"What are you thinking?"

"That I need to go over my notes on the flower plan for the house and gazebo, and then review what we know so far about the case."

"We've done all of that, Kayla. The night before a big op is time to rest and sleep as much as possible. You don't know when you'll get rest again."

"Why are you so sure we'll get the murderer tomorrow?"

"Because Tony Charbonneau may suspect that the information Meredith had was copied. Meredith was a perfectionist and threatened him that she was going to the police unless he came clean. Someone that smart wouldn't *not* make a copy. He has no idea that we have it, but it's enough to make him act out. He'll want to deal with whomever he thinks has the information."

"Or have one of his thugs do it for him."

"Right."

They were at her shop where she maneuvered the van up the alley and to the back of it. "How will we get to your place?"

"My car is around the corner."

"You think of everything, Rio."

Two hours later she sat at Rio's kitchen table sipping herbal tea and going through the notes Rio had on the case. She considered it a small victory that he'd let her look at his private notes. Talking the case over was one thing but sharing his personal theories and hunches meant more to her than a dinner out on the town. She giggled.

"I didn't realize the Charbonneaus were amusing." He drank a big mug of warm milk as he leaned against the granite counter. A grey T-shirt stretched across his chest and pajama bottoms with Spider-Man printed on them somehow looked sexy on him.

"Where did you get the Spidey pj's?"

He glanced down. "My sisters. They're always getting me silly stuff at Christmas."

"Do you ever go back to Texas for the holidays?"

He shook his head. "No. My family's all here now. We moved after my grandfather died. My uncle was already in central Pennsylvania, so it was an easy thing for my mother to do. My *abuelita* had passed by then…" He took another gulp of his milk before he leveled his brown eyes on her. "No distractions. Focus. What were you laughing at?"

"I was thinking about what a big deal it is for you to share your case notes with anyone, especially me. And for me, it's a huge gift. Thank you. This is more meaningful to me than if you took me out for a lobster dinner with champagne." She'd almost said *romantic dinner*. Not where her mind, or Rio's, needed to go tonight.

"I understand." He was perfectly still and she wanted to get up from the table and wrap her arms around his waist, get him to open up more about his childhood, his teenage years, what led him to be a cop. But they had work to do and she had to keep her head on straight. Figuring out what she wanted to do with her feelings for Rio couldn't be done while working on her first case for Trail Hikers.

"We need to rest, Kayla. Let's call it a night." He eased off the counter, turned and rinsed his mug. Kayla stood up and closed his laptop. "Thanks, Rio. I'll see you in the morning. Good night."

"Good night, Kayla."

She went to the guest room, her body aching with need and desire for him. There were so many reasons to quell her longing for Rio, from the fact that they didn't need the distraction, as he'd said, to the reality that Rio wasn't a man to mess with. If she gave herself to him again, it had to come with something more permanent. A commitment.

That word didn't elicit thoughts of a nightmarish life stifled by boredom, or a vanilla life in a small town in the middle of nowhere. Instead, a small thrill ran through her and made her think that maybe, just maybe, she and Rio could make a go of it.

After they solved the case.

Chapter 17

Rio woke to the sound of dripping rain the morning of the wedding. As he lay in his bed he couldn't help but want Kayla here, next to him. There were times he hated being so damn professional. Except for the total lapse of sanity on Kayla's stairs, which he was grateful as hell for, he'd steered away from too much physical connection.

The woman already has your heart.

He sat up, almost hitting his knees against the nightstand as he swung his legs around. Where the hell had that thought come from?

From the same place as the uncontrollable urge to tear off her clothes in her foyer had. Last night had been rough. He'd fought his primal urge to make love to her on his maple kitchen table. She'd looked so damn hot as she'd studied his notes.

He was losing it. Since when did anyone look sexy working on a laptop? And when she'd commented on his Spider-Man bottoms, he'd wanted to invite her to take them off and let him show her what a superhero he could be.

He stumbled into the bathroom and took his usual four-minute shower, shaved and was in the kitchen with coffee perking by five. Kayla needed to be at the Charbonneaus' by eight, so he'd probably have a couple of hours to himself until she woke up. He'd been surprised by how quickly she got ready in the mornings. As if she'd been born into law enforcement.

He opened his laptop and prepared to sink himself into the case, searching as always for the missed clue, the overlooked detail that could yield pay dirt. The murderer.

"Rio. Good morning." She stood at the counter in her pajamas, her hair mussed but her eyes bright and an anticipatory expression on her face. "It's takedown or bust today, isn't it?"

Ignoring her reference to the case, he shut his laptop. "There's fresh coffee for you. Creamer is…you know where the creamer is." He couldn't stand up and pour her a cup of the fresh brew, not without her noticing what he wanted at the moment. His erection strained against his cargo pants and he wondered how soft her mouth would feel against his.

"Thanks." She helped herself and he took advantage of the view of her ass in her short pajama bottoms.

Tight and curvy. "You working on the case?" She shot the question over her shoulder, oblivious to his morning sexual fantasies.

Morning sex. They hadn't had that since they'd dated. And it was hard to classify it as morning or nighttime sex then, as when they'd been together it had been a constant need they'd both been eager to fulfill during the wee hours.

"I was going over some of my notes."

"You're always on a case, aren't you?" She pulled out the chair across from him and sat down, but not before he had a full view of her hard nipples pressed against her knit tank top. Maybe she was thinking about morning sex, too.

"It's my job. I can't leave it at the office."

She sipped the hot liquid, her full lips on his heavy-duty ceramic mug. At her silence he met her gaze and realized she knew exactly what he was thinking about as he stared at her mouth on the cup. She licked her lips. He could see that her pupils were dilated despite the bright kitchen light.

"Kayla, this is a tense time. It's natural to feel, um…"

She laughed.

"Why, Detective Ortega, is that a blush on your face? I don't think I've ever seen you speechless before."

He leaned back and reassessed. Kayla knew exactly what was passing between them across the table. It was a hell of a lot more than the stress of the case. It was the hope that they'd be successful and take down not just a murderer, but the entire posse of losers who were posing as upright citizens. Starting with Mickey and Tony Charbonneau.

"We have a lot on our plate. I've found one bite at a time is usually the best way to handle cases like this, but with what's happened so far we should expect the unexpected."

"We've gone over every possible angle with Claudia umpteen times, Rio. We're ready."

"Almost."

It was Kayla's turn to blush.

The jolt of caffeine from the coffee only fueled her arousal. Rio Ortega was the sexiest man she'd ever known, and living under his roof the past week had become both familiar and excruciating.

"Don't tease and flirt now, Rio. We have a job to do." He'd been the one to make sure they didn't cross the invisible boundaries they'd erected. She couldn't call it a mistake anymore, what they'd done last week. And she didn't regret it. But now she understood better than she had before her Trail Hikers training that they needed their space to prepare. To stay safe.

"I'm not teasing, Kayla. I've been doing all I can to keep my hands off you for the better part of a week, and the thought of having to wire you without being able to touch you the way I want to is driving me crazy."

"How crazy do you feel?" She purposefully let her voice remain low and gravelly. She could flirt back. Let him feel how hot and bothered she was, living under his roof, sharing his kitchen, his space. As if the time in between when they'd stopped seeing one another and now didn't exist.

Except they'd stayed away from the bedroom. A laugh erupted from her and she had to put down her mug before she spilled coffee on the polished wood table. "I'm sorry but I was thinking about how careful we've been to stay away from each other, especially at night and in the morning."

"When we're coming from or going to bed." His face was set in grim lines as if he was enduring torture and she leaned over and ran her fingers down his smooth cheek. He'd already shaved.

"Yes, yet when we lost control, we…"

"Weren't even in the bedroom." His hand came up and clasped hers, tugging, pulling her up and around the table, where he pulled her down onto his lap.

Kayla meant to simply sit down on his lap, but she saw his erection through his pants and without hesitation straddled him. The heavy wooden kitchen chair easily took both their weight and she exclaimed at the sheer pleasure the close contact jolted through her.

Rio drove his hands through her hair and grasped the back of her neck as if she was drowning and he had to give her resuscitation. Instead of air, he pressed his tongue into her mouth and Kayla lost all hope of using the extra hours of wakefulness to prepare for the wedding.

They were preparing in a different way.

Her need matched his kiss for kiss, squeeze for squeeze. Rio rocked his pelvis under hers and she shuddered at the near release it brought, as if they were teens experimenting through their clothing.

"Rio, let's take our clothes off."

"No talking." He grasped her hands and entwined his fingers with hers, placing their hands in the space between both of their chests. She felt his heartbeat match her own and the turn-on was more than she could handle. Pressing her lips to his, she kissed him as if it was the last time she'd be able to.

Rio held her hip and lifted her off him. Before she could protest at the lack of contact, he had her pajama shorts down around her feet. She unzipped his cargos and reached for him as his pants fell to meet her bottoms.

Rio had her tank top up, off and over her head, and she knew she'd find it somewhere strange later as she did the same with his T-shirt.

"We have to stop meeting like this." Her words came out in short pants and she shook with want. He stood next to her, his shoulders blocking her view of the French doors that led to his backyard.

"Rio, your neighbors."

"Screw 'em." He kissed her hard and brought her hips up against his erection with his hands cupped under her buttocks, kneading and caressing her with a skill she wanted to get on her knees and thank God for. "They're not up yet, anyway." With no further conversation, he bent down and lifted her into his arms.

"Rio, this isn't going to tire you out for work today, is it?" She looked up at his face as he walked down the short hall to his bedroom. Not the guest room, where she'd been staying, but his room, his sanctuary.

As if being with Rio wasn't enough, once he placed her on his bed, she was inundated with his scent on the sheets and her desire peaked from the extra stimulation of her senses. As Rio lay down next to her, she rose on all fours and started kissing him at his neck, his shoulders, his chest. Bracing her hands on his shoulders, she straddled him again, but this time didn't allow their pelvises to meet. Instead she kept inching down his torso, licking and kissing his hard abs as her hands massaged his shoulders.

"You're killing me here, Kayla." His words were punctuated by sharp intakes of breath and she let her power over him make her lovemaking more ardent, more intense. When she got to his erection and lowered her mouth to it, the groan of satisfaction from Rio was worth every minute of keeping her own satisfaction at bay. She sucked and kissed and licked until Rio took hold of her hips and moved her to the side.

No words as he suckled each of her breasts with tenderness and passion, his fingers inside her, moving, making her hips gyrate in a desperate attempt to reach the climax his lovemaking always promised.

Rio chuckled against her stomach, her belly, lower. She moaned. When his tongue dipped into her belly button and then kept going, she ran her fingers through his hair and urged his head lower. Again Rio interlaced his fingers with hers and held her hands to either side as he dived into her center, his tongue further arousing her swollen and wet insides until she screamed his name at the peak of her climax. As she came back to planet earth, Rio didn't wait. As soon as he had a condom on, he was on top of her, moving over her, and entered her with their eyes connected. She couldn't keep her eyes open for long but it was long enough to see that this was more than lust for him, too.

Nothing sounded sweeter to her than Rio's hoarse utterance of her name as he came and brought her with him, their bodies slick, hot and completely engulfed in bliss.

After several minutes, she felt Rio stir and raise himself over and to her side, resting on his back. She curled into him and traced lazy circles on his chest, loving how completely relaxed his profile appeared in the lightening room.

"Sun's up." She kissed his shoulder.

He opened one eye and snorted. "I won't be again for a while, thanks to you."

They lay together for a few moments longer, until Rio's deep exhalation alerted her to what they both needed to do today.

Catch a killer.

Cynthia's wedding day had dawned damp and drizzly, but the sun was starting to peek out from behind big white and grey fluffy clouds as she drove to the mayor's house. Kayla wasn't worried about the ceremony, since she'd arranged to have the path from the back door of the house to the gazebo covered, and the gazebo was large enough to hold the entire wedding party along with a handful of guests, and keep them dry. The other guests would be given white umbrellas as they arrived at the house, to keep the appearance of the ceremony uniform and "tasteful, not tacky" as Cynthia had requested.

Being wired wasn't as uncomfortable as she'd expected, thanks to the Trail Hikers having up-to-date technology. Some of the equipment wasn't even on the commercial market yet. She'd have to take off her clothes for anyone to see the superthin wires and tiny microphones. Rio had wanted to hook her up with two-way comms with SVPD but she'd declined. She didn't have the training for it.

SVPD was providing security for the event, since as far as the public knew, the mayor was conceivably at risk in light of Meredith's murder.

Rio was in an unmarked police van in front of the house, listening to Kayla's feed. She placed a large basket of extra flowers on the back porch, hoping she wouldn't need them. The bridal party's flowers were in the refrigeration unit of her van.

"I don't see why you're so upset. He'll show up. The men went out for nightcaps after the rehearsal dinner." Cynthia's voice wafted out of the open door and Kayla caught a glimpse of Gloria walking into the dining room in a bathrobe. The woman even ate breakfast at the formal dining table?

"It's not like him. He's very prompt and is always at your father's side. And he's your godfather—he has to be here." Gloria's voice was high-pitched and reflected worry as Kayla eased closer to the door without putting herself in their line of sight. They knew she'd be out here, but perhaps didn't realize she could overhear them.

"What's got you so wound up, Gloria? Mickey isn't in the wedding. Even if he doesn't show up, Dad can survive without him today. My wedding has nothing to do with the mayor's office."

"Don't kid yourself." Gloria's stunning retort was as sharp as if she'd slapped Cynthia.

"Let's not get ugly on *my* wedding day, Gloria. It's important to my father that it's perfect for me, remember." Was Cynthia warning Gloria?

"Yes, yes, we'll keep it perfect for you. But you need to learn some hard truths about adulthood, Cynthia. Charles wouldn't be marrying you unless you fit his résumé, too."

"We're in love, Gloria."

"Save it for the wedding guests. You don't need to BS me."

"No, I suppose I don't." Dishes clattered as they served themselves food. Kayla didn't think their voices would reach the microphones nestled between her breasts, but she'd make sure to memorize everything they said to pass to Rio and Claudia. The Charbonneaus, whether by marriage or blood, were a miserable, conniving lot. It was a matter of time before one of them slipped up and revealed the way to the murderer.

"That's enough, Cynthia." Gloria's censure was sharper.

"Excuse me. You're only six years older than me, Gloria. I don't take orders or reprimands from you. Let's keep this civil for as long as we can. And trust me, you're in no place to tell anyone what to do." Did Cynthia know about Gloria and Mickey's affair?

"I'd say that the line for civility was crossed long ago. Look over your shoulder—it's way back there, about the time I married your father."

Meow, meow.

"That's enough, ladies." Tony Charbonneau's cajoling voice sliced through their bickering. "What on earth is upsetting you both on this great day? My baby girl is going to marry a wonderful man." Silence, other than the sound of cutlery, fell inside the house. Kayla stood to stretch her quads as she'd been crouching next to the flower basket for several minutes. A soft footfall was her only warning before the back doors opened wider and Cynthia strode through. Kayla grabbed a handful of flowers and made as if to add more to the balcony.

Cynthia's stare would have made her blood run cold only a week ago. Now, with Trail Hikers training behind her and an automatic weapon hidden on a calf holster under her pant leg, Kayla stood and stared back at Cynthia.

"What are you doing here? Aren't you supposed to be getting the gazebo ready?" She looked at Kayla as though Kayla was a family servant rather than a professional working in the twenty-first century.

"The gazebo's ready. I'm finishing up with this railing. I'm here if you need anything before I give the flowers to your attendants."

"Why are you on the porch?" Cynthia looked back

at the threshold she'd just passed, then again at Kayla. "What did you overhear?"

"What's to overhear? I've been on the phone with my assistant and placing the flowers. Did I miss something you need done, Cynthia?"

Cynthia Charbonneau's beauty, if you could call it that, was entirely due to her father's bankroll. And that meant it was highly likely that the funds he'd been embezzling from Silver Valley had paid for top-of-the-line skin treatments, spa time and probably a collagen injection or two. But as the woman stared at Kayla, there was no attractiveness. Only an ugly energy reminiscent of feral cats when they were about to attack.

"I don't need anything else from you. Just stay out of the way." Kayla knew Cynthia's words reached Rio's ears and wondered what he made of her tyrannical tone. Probably thought what Kayla did. That Cynthia had been spoiled her entire life.

"When are the groom and his attendants expected? My assistant is bringing the boutonnieres separately."

Cynthia waved her hand as if her soon-to-be-husband was no more than an accessory. "Charles will show up an hour before, no sooner. There's no reason for him to. They had a fun time after the party. I wouldn't be surprised if he is hungover, along with the rest of the men." Cynthia didn't seem to care her husband might be hungover on their wedding day. She didn't care about the wedding as long as she got a high-powered groom out of it.

"Are you excited about graduating from law school

next week, too? You have a lot of milestones happening in such a short time."

Cynthia's smirk made it clear that Kayla was the florist, damn it, not her therapist. "It's not pressing on me. I'll graduate, pass the bar and start my law career under Charles's wing. No one can say anything since he'll be my husband." She laughed. "I know I'm not the usual blushing bride. Let's just say I'm more practical. The people, people like you, in Silver Valley are ludicrous. You'll be happy as a florist, probably get married and have babies. That's not for me. I've known since I was a small girl that I'm headed for bigger things."

Gloria stared at Tony. She knew her husband was capable of underhanded business. Sure, he broke the law here and there, but it was always for the good of the people he served. Mickey helped him with that.

Mickey.

He'd ignored her last night at the rehearsal dinner. Of course he did. He'd been there as Cynthia's godfather, but it was obvious he was only there for Tony. To do whatever Tony needed him to do.

"You're awfully quiet, Gloria. Did you have your share of vodka last night, too?" Tony grinned at her, his forkful of scrambled eggs and smoked salmon halfway to his smug mouth. His lips were thin and tight, not generous and sweet like Mickey's.

"Where's Mickey, Tony? I thought he was coming over to help you get ready and to keep everyone calm."

Tony shook his head. "I told him to sleep in, take it

easy. He's done enough for me these past weeks. Why are you so worried about him, Gloria?"

Tony's question was scary and too close to the truth, but as she looked at his open expression, his tired eyes, she realized it was just her guilt.

"No, no. It's wedding-day jitters, that's all. Honey, you know I just want whatever's best for Cynthia."

"I know, sweetheart." He chewed. "Tell you what. After she's married and on her way to her own life, I'll take you on a nice trip, okay? You want Atlantic City or maybe even Vegas?"

"Oh, Tony, that would be so fun!"

He pointed his fork at her. "Okay. So, just stay calm and collected today and remember, it's Cynthia's day. Everything else can wait."

Gloria thought a trip was a good idea, but she'd rather go with Mickey.

Chapter 18

"Any questions?"

Rio looked at the assembled group of SVPD and other local law-enforcement officers who were working the Charbonneau wedding with him. Half would be in uniform, providing legit security for the political figures. It wasn't questioned by the mayor, who'd fallen for Rio's explanation that because Meredith had been murdered, it was imperative that they keep Tony safe, as well as his family. That they were all potential targets. Tony had eaten it up.

"No, sir." A collective response, which Rio expected. They'd already gone over every possible aspect of the takedown ad infinitum for the past seventy-two hours.

"Thank you, ladies and gentlemen. Let's do this."

Rio walked out of the briefing room before the crowd dispersed, wanting to speak to Colt Todd alone before he went to the unmarked van where he'd check with the comms team to make sure all was up and running with Kayla's equipment. For all he knew she'd already captured some pertinent evidence.

"Head on in, Rio. I'm grabbing more coffee." Colt was only a minute behind Rio. He took his spot behind the large desk and motioned for Rio to sit down. "Are we ready to do this, Rio? How's Kayla holding up?"

"Yes, sir, and she's doing well. I'm confident she'll get whatever she can from the Charbonneaus, but too much of this relies on luck for my liking."

"It's not luck, it's the result of hard work and timing. We have no other options at this point. You'll bring in the mayor if he shows any hint of bolting, and definitely once the wedding is over if nothing happens before then. He'll go to jail for embezzlement and fraud if nothing else."

"I want him for murder."

"I do, too, but all we have is circumstantial. Anything new on Mickey?"

"No, no match on weapons, no prints. He says he was at home the night of the attempt on Kayla. We have Kayla's testimony that it was him the night of Meredith's murder, but even she can only identify his voice. She never saw his face in the dark that night and never saw the shooter when they aimed at her."

Colt frowned. "The bullets were the same, though. It's the same weapon."

"Right. But Ippolito doesn't have a license for the

weapon that fired those bullets, and when we searched his place and auto there was nothing. *Nada*."

"We'll force them out, Rio. If nothing else it'll be a wedding of gangsters like no one's seen since *The Godfather*."

"Judge Blackwell isn't a gangster."

Colt shook his head. "No, he's not. And he's a good friend. I've tried to talk to him about Cynthia, but he won't hear a word against her. But I guess sometimes we can't help who we fall for, can we, Rio?" Colt looked at him and Rio felt a jolt of realization up his spine.

"Yes, sir."

"I'm not talking about you and Kayla, Rio. Although that would be appropriate, I'm sure. How's it been with her at your house?"

"We've managed." This morning they'd done a whole lot of managing. He hid his grin.

"I like the idea of you two. You've needed to settle down for a while now. Maybe after the case you two can make it official. Now get out of here and keep me in the loop. I'll be checking in with comms regularly."

"Yes, sir." Rio stood and left. His mind wasn't on the comms team. It was on getting in touch with Kayla and making sure she was doing okay. He reached into his pocket for his phone and stopped. He couldn't text her. Not now, as she was in the middle of the wedding prep. And the middle of an op. He trusted and admired Kayla, but at this moment he wished like hell that her talents weren't placing her dangerously close to a killer.

* * *

Rio rapped quickly on the back door of the comms van, parked on the block behind the mayor's house, hidden in between two large lilac bushes.

The door opened slowly and Claudia smiled at him. "Come on in. I hope you brought doughnuts."

He saw she was joking as there was already a bag of pastries on the tiny counter in the vehicle, along with a carton of take-out coffee.

"Nika." Nika Pasczenko served as SVPD's top comms officer.

"Detective Ortega. Nothing yet, just wedding chatter. The mic's good, though. Picking up just about everything that Kayla is hearing."

"Good." He looked at Claudia. They were hunched on tiny stools in close confines. She looked more awake than any of them, of course. Claudia was always "on."

"Nika tells me you two worked the same beat before you were promoted to detective."

"Yeah, we had our times, didn't we?" She'd been his partner and a damn good one. He'd been as surprised as anyone that he'd been promoted before her. Only seniority had made that happen, he was sure.

"I was telling Claudia that you were the best partner. You never treated me any differently because I'm a woman. I was just an officer."

He squirmed at the compliment. "You are an officer, Nika. The best."

"Don't look so uncomfortable. Take the praise." Claudia patted his shoulder.

They listened to Kayla as she spoke with Jenny, suggesting where fresh flowers needed to be placed, pointing out where some blooms had wilted in the rain.

"Has she talked to the mayor or Gloria yet?"

"No, but she's talked to Cynthia. Nothing significant. Here." Nika passed him her headset. His cell phone buzzed.

"Ortega."

"Mickey's dead." Colt Todd's voice was grim and the implication of the two words was like a sucker punch.

"How? Where?"

"A fisherman found his body on the bank of Conodoguinet Creek early this morning. Maybe drowned, but we need the tox report to know what got him there in the first place. The coroner suspects intoxication."

"Maybe he felt guilty over killing Meredith." As he spoke he knew it wasn't true. Mickey Ippolito was a thug from way back. He'd do Tony Charbonneau's bidding without a twinge of guilt.

"Doubt it. There were drag marks and the grass on either side of the dirt path was flattened, but no footprints. He was either dead or unconscious before he was put in the water." Colt paused. "You thinking what I'm thinking?"

"We've narrowed down who killed Meredith."

"Right. It likely wasn't Mickey."

Rio ended the call and swore.

"I take it the mayor's assistant is dead?" Claudia's eyes pierced his mental noise.

"Yes. They found his body on a creek bank this morning."

"Foul play?"

"From the looks of it."

"Mayor Charbonneau would have every reason to take Mickey out if he thought Mickey posed a risk." Claudia was thinking aloud, a common way they brainstormed cases.

"Or if he thought Mickey was going to take off with the funds, but Mickey didn't strike me as an accounting mastermind."

Claudia gave one short shake of her head. "Tony would never trust the security passwords for his money to anyone else."

"Except Gloria." He didn't believe that, either, though. "No, he wouldn't trust Gloria. She's his trophy wife, period. He puts his grown daughter's needs over hers from all we've seen. That speaks volumes."

"What about—"

"Cynthia." They said her name in unison.

As if on cue, Cynthia's voice came over the audio feed, which Nika had turned up.

"Really, Gloria, you amuse me. It's my day today and you're still trying to get all of the attention for yourself."

"Don't you need to go get ready? Your makeup will take a while."

Cynthia laughed. "Oh, Gloria, you have no idea how

happy I am that you're here with me today. No matter our differences. Family is family, after all."

An hour before the ceremony, the flowers were as close to perfect as Kayla and Jenny were going to get them. The rain had stopped and a lingering mist gave the backyard and gazebo area a fairy-tale feeling.

"It's perfect if you look at it with an artist's eye." Jenny had a wistful expression. "Although Gloria and Cynthia Charbonneau aren't really the artistic type, are they?"

"No, they're not. Let's get these extra stems and supplies out of here, and we'll bring in the boutonnieres. The bouquets will wait until the last minute."

"Kayla!" Gloria's sharp voice carried across the sloping lawn and Kayla turned.

"Jeez, does she think you're a dog?" Jenny's disgust twisted her mouth into a sneer that rivaled a comic villain's. Kayla suppressed the urge to laugh—she didn't want to start trouble with Gloria.

"What do you need?" On the porch Gloria's fully dressed and made-up state, complete with makeup, made her look like a C-list Hollywood actress. "Are you taking the photos now?"

"Yes, and the photographer needs Cynthia's bouquet. Now."

Kayla ignored the last word and went straight for the van, where she'd parked it alongside the house on a small driveway. Jenny was ahead of her and handed her Cynthia's bouquet from the back refrigeration section.

"Thanks, Jenny."

Kayla accepted the flowers and looked into the middle of the pure white blossoms—Cynthia hadn't wanted any color but white. That was what she was getting, along with a tiny microphone similar to the one that was taped to Kayla. Rio and Claudia would be able to pick up what Kayla couldn't.

She rounded the back again and went into the house. Remains of a beautiful breakfast were on the sideboard and an empty champagne bottle was in a silver bucket, the ice melting around it. From the sounds of laughter as she neared the stairs, the bridal party had enjoyed the bubbly.

"Up here." Sylvia hurried down the stairs and took the bouquet from Kayla. "She's pitching a fit but her friends are keeping her happy enough."

"Anything I can do?"

Sylvia started to shake her head, then paused. "Yes. Come upstairs if you don't mind, and make sure that these are exactly how Cynthia wants them."

Kayla got it. Sylvia didn't want to be on the receiving end of any displeasure from Cynthia. Because that would mean dealing with an annoyed Gloria. No matter how strained the ties between Gloria and her stepdaughter, Gloria seemed to bend over backward to keep her happy.

To keep the husband she was cheating on happy.

The bridal party surrounded Cynthia and at first all Kayla saw were the pale lavender bridesmaids dresses. The group of five parted to allow her through, revealing Cynthia in a froth of white taffeta and silk.

"Oh." Kayla caught her breath. "You look beautiful."

As her bridal party murmured their agreement, Kayla kept her impression to herself. Her surprise hadn't been at Cynthia's beautiful image, not that she wasn't a beautiful bride.

It was the dress. It was incongruous with the hard-edged, career-driven Cynthia. Latin-themed, it resembled a flamenco dancer's hourglass cut, off one shoulder, and very, very frilly around the hips and hem. No doubt the Charbonneaus had spared no expense for the gown, which Kayla thought was the true shame of it all.

"These are a little bigger than we talked about, aren't they?" Gloria asked, eyeing the bouquet against Cynthia's gown.

"They're a perfect balance for the wedding gown and overall theme." The photographer spoke up, and Kayla wanted to kiss him at the sheer adulation that poured from Cynthia's expression at his praise.

"Yes, you're right, they are." Cynthia never missed a chance to cut down Gloria, either.

"When will the groom and groomsmen be here? We have their flowers ready," Kayla said to Sylvia as Gloria and Cynthia were posing for the camera.

"They should be here any minute. We expected them downstairs an hour ago, in the backyard, but one of them isn't there yet."

"Oh?"

"Yes, the mayor's downstairs trying to sort it out."

"Okay, then, I'll go talk to him."

Sylvia placed a cool hand on her forearm. "Careful. He's in a mood about it all."

The warning wasn't expected, especially from Sylvia, with whom she'd had little interaction save for Gloria's weekly flowers. Kayla looked into her eyes and saw exhaustion and perhaps genuine concern. Working for the Charbonneaus was wearing on her.

"Thank you. I'll step lightly."

She darted out of the room and down the stairs, figuring the mayor's office had to be somewhere off the main foyer, near Gloria's. A deep male voice drew her to a closed oak door, where she paused.

"Just come over without him, then. He'll show up."

Silence.

She rapped twice, then asked, "May I come in? It's the florist."

"Come in, come in." Tony opened the door before she did and offered her a rueful smile. "I'm trying to track down one of the groomsmen and not having any luck. He probably tied one on last night and is sleeping it off with his phone turned off." He worked the cuff links on his tuxedo. "It's not like him, though."

"Which groomsman is it?"

He shot her an assessing glance, and in that beat she knew he didn't see her as a threat.

"Cynthia's godfather, Mickey Ippolito. She's going to be heartbroken if he doesn't get here in time."

"This often happens at weddings. I've seen the groom as well as the bride show up at the very last minute, even late. There's the exhaustion from the preparation, the rehearsal dinner, often the drinking afterward. Maybe some of them went out to another bar after the dinner was over?"

"Maybe. Where's Cynthia? Still getting her picture taken?"

"Yes, she's upstairs with Gloria and the bridal party. The photographer will need you soon, too." Kayla had been around countless weddings and they all seemed to have the same timing, the same rhythm to them. Although this wedding had deadly tension added to the mix.

"Please excuse me. Did you get anything to eat? Help yourself." The mayor strode out of the office and she turned as though she was headed to the dining room. Instead she went back into his office as soon as he was up the stairs.

Kayla wasn't sure what she was looking for, but her brief training had taught her to exploit each and every opportunity to gather information and intelligence. She looked over the masculine room, loaded with thick hardcover books from floor to ceiling. She couldn't say why, but she doubted Tony had read many, if any, of the books. Everything about the Charbonneaus was for show.

A cursory sweep of the office revealed nothing, until she saw a familiar pattern on the corner of one of the shelves behind his desk.

Would he be that stupid?

She stepped forward and pulled out the file folder, and started to narrate what she was doing in a very low, quiet voice. Rio needed to know where she was.

"I've found the same folder I saw fall out of Meredith's briefcase, the same pattern I saw on a file in Gloria's office. I'm in the mayor's home office. The folder is—" she opened it "—empty. There's a small pocket meant for a flash drive but it's empty, too." Disappointment welled and she felt foolish. "I'm putting back the file." She shoved it between the two books, where she'd noticed it, and stood up straight.

"What are you doing?" Cynthia stood in the doorway, her angry expression at odds with her princess wedding attire.

"I didn't hear you come down the stairs."

"I took the back stairs, through the kitchen. Answer my question."

"I'm waiting for the groomsmen to arrive. My assistant is getting their boutonnieres ready. Your father told me to wait for them." A little white lie never hurt.

Cynthia continued to stare at her for a full moment until the clamor of the rest of the bridal party distracted her. "We need this space to take photos of my father and me. You have to leave."

Kayla smiled and waited for Cynthia to clear the threshold before walking out of the room. Her heart was pounding. She needed to get a grip.

It was going to be a long day and the vows hadn't even been exchanged yet.

Chapter 19

"We're doing this now, Rio." Colt Todd stood with Rio behind the comms van, his hands on his hips.

"I think we could get some more intel if we let them stew a bit more. They don't need to know Mickey's dead, not yet. I want to hear everyone's reaction when he doesn't show."

Colt shook his head, but before he could say anything more, Claudia stepped out of the van. "Contemplating the fine morning, gentlemen?"

Colt actually smiled and Rio stared. He wasn't used to seeing the man express much overt emotion. Was there something to it? Although Claudia was attractive, he couldn't see them together.

Could he?

Damn it, but he was seeing romance everywhere

since he'd decided he was going to talk to Kayla when this was all over. They had too much between them to let it go because she was afraid of commitment. He had been, too, but life was too short.

"We're disagreeing on when to notify the mayor that his assistant is dead."

"From what I just heard on Kayla's feed, he's also the bride's godfather. We can't be certain who exactly is our suspect."

"Right, but it's not fair to have a wedding without him there, and them all wondering why not." Colt was pragmatic. "Plus it's not our problem about the timing. It's life."

"Okay, go ahead and tell them. Be alert. If you can have Kayla there, even better."

"Roger." Rio didn't look at his boss as they fell into step together on the sidewalk, passing early arriving guests. As they weren't in uniform, they wouldn't cause a stir, not yet.

Once in the house Rio spotted Kayla in the foyer, attending to a groomsman's flower on his lapel. She looked up at him and her soft smile was pure joy. She quickly put her professional mask back in place and finished pinning the thick, heavily taped stem.

They found the mayor in the kitchen, sipping black coffee and on his cell phone. When he saw Colt he looked him over, as if wondering why he was at his daughter's wedding in a sport jacket and not a suit.

"Good morning. We need to talk. Privately." Colt didn't wait for Tony to end his conversation.

Tony put his phone in his tuxedo jacket pocket. "Colt. What's this about?"

"Privately." Colt didn't budge.

"Very well, come on. We don't have a lot of time." Tony led them to his office, where Rio looked around until he spied the folder Kayla had been talking about on the feed. The pink-and-purple flowery design stood out like a sore thumb amongst manila folders and books.

Rio closed the doors behind them and stayed silent, allowing Colt to tell Tony the bad news.

"Mickey Ippolito is dead."

Tony Charbonneau paled, then flushed, then sat down hard on his luxurious office chair. It groaned under the force of his action. His hands started shaking and he shook his head in disbelief. "Come again?"

"He drowned in the creek. In barely a foot of water. Do you happen to know if he was drunk last night?"

"No, not at all. Sure, we were all having a few, celebrating, but…" He trailed off and pinched the bridge of his nose with his fingers. "I can't tell Cynthia. Not today. It's too special."

"Might you want to postpone the wedding?" Rio asked.

"Absolutely not. This is Cynthia's day and it needs to go forward. She and Charles have their lives planned, and if she doesn't marry him now, it will have to wait until she passes the bar. She doesn't have any time to spare in her schedule." He frowned. "Sometimes it can take two or three times, more. Cynthia's a good student, but lots of smart kids have to repeat the bar."

"We'll leave the decision to you as to when you tell her, but we'll have to question everyone as soon as possible."

"You're not going to question her on her wedding day!"

"Yes, we are. It's procedure. We can do it before the wedding or right after. You decide."

Tony stared at his hands on the leather-framed blotter. "I don't want her upset for the service. I'll tell her he drank too much, if she asks. She may not. He's her godfather, though, I..." His voice cracked and Rio thought that Tony had genuine affection for Mickey. Too bad they were both criminals.

"What's with that folder?" Rio asked, catching the mayor exactly where he wanted to. Vulnerable.

"What folder?" Tony frowned and looked at Rio.

"The one behind you, with the flowers on it."

Tony looked behind him and shrugged. "I'm not sure what you're getting at. There's a lot of files back there."

"You know which one I'm talking about." Rio felt Colt shift next to him, but his boss remained silent. Even if Colt thought Rio was chasing rainbows and unicorns, he'd keep quiet in front of a suspect. Rio would pay hell, however, if it turned out he didn't know what he was doing.

But he was pretty sure he did.

"What?" Tony kept up the angry pose. "You come in here and tell me my friend is dead, and now you're asking about a manila folder? Is Mickey really dead or are you shitting me to get your case solved?"

As soon as he said the words, Tony's bluster faded.

He obviously realized his mistake. "Here, take it. What's so special about it, anyhow?" He pulled out the flowery folder and threw it on his desk.

Rio opened it and saw it was empty just as Kayla described. "What was in this pocket, Tony? May I remind you that you are speaking to two sworn officers of the law."

Tony sat stone-silent for several seconds. He looked at the folder. At Rio. His expression when he looked at Colt was apologetic. "I should have come to you, or at least the town, sooner. I've long suspected Mickey was up to something, maybe even in cahoots with Meredith. When she was found dead, I asked him what he knew about it, but he swore he didn't kill her. That he'd never do that. I believed him."

"Why would he kill her, Tony?" Colt asked, playing more of the good-guy routine.

"Because she found some files he'd been keeping and she interpreted them as proof of illegal doings."

"Such as?" Rio was curious to know what Tony would make up on the spot. No way would this thug who played at being a mayor admit his culpability.

"I think it was something to do with registering some voters illegally in the last election. It doesn't matter because I won by a landslide. I didn't need any voter fraud to get elected." His smug complacency in the face of the news that his lifetime friend and partner in crime was dead, and his ability to blame him for the mayor's wrongdoing, didn't shock Rio. It threatened to enrage him, however, and if not for his experience and training, he'd be inclined to arrest the mayor right now, in front of all the wedding guests.

"Did you have any reason to want Mickey dead, Tony?" Colt asked the question as though he was asking about fly-fishing, one of his favorite pastimes.

"Are you kidding me? He was like a brother to me. My best friend for years. The godfather to my daughter. How can you ask this now?"

"Did you know he was having an affair with your wife?"

"Do you mean my ex-wife?" Tony looked incredulous.

"No. Your current wife." Rio kept chipping at his defenses. Even sociopaths could slip up.

"Gloria?" Tony threw back his head and laughed. "Gloria and Mickey?" He kept laughing, then looked at them, stone sober. "Never."

A quick knock, then the woman herself appeared.

"Tony, we're getting ready to start the service. It's a damn shame Mickey's not here." She looked at Colt, then Rio, as if just realizing they weren't groomsmen. Her recognition registered and she stiffened. "What are you two doing here?"

"They're paying respects for Cynthia's wedding, Gloria." Tony stood up. "What do you think they're doing here? They're running the security today. We don't want any fruitcakes ruining my baby's wedding. Go on ahead, I'll be right there. We were almost done." Gloria left and Tony shut the door behind her, leaving his hand on the doorknob as he turned back to them.

"We'll tell everyone else after the wedding ceremony, and you can ask questions as needed then. And I swear, if either of you ever accuse my wife of screwing around on me again, I'll make sure your badges are gone so fast you won't know what hit you until you're in the unemployment line." He opened the door. "I trust you can see yourselves out."

"Not so fast, Tony." Colt smiled. "We're staying for the wedding. To make sure the security is tight and all."

The mayor of Silver Valley growled at them as he turned and left.

"Do you think it was him?" Colt murmured to Rio as they smiled at arriving guests. They stood apart from the general crowd, between the gazebo and back porch.

"I don't know. He seemed genuinely surprised that Mickey was dead. But he knows more, I'm certain. Like who Mickey would have left with, if he was too drunk to drive."

"Yeah." Colt stretched his neck. "Did you see the food they're setting up inside? They're having a lunch buffet after the ceremony and the big dinner tonight. No one's going hungry at this wedding."

"What looked good to you?"

"The seafood risotto. It's from Veronique's Café, in Harrisburg."

"I didn't know you got to the other side of the river much, boss."

Colt laughed. "I do have some free time, and I enjoy a good meal as much as anyone. You know I've been to Paris, right?"

"No, I didn't." Rio never asked Colt about his personal life. It just wasn't done in the precinct.

"Yup, spent two weeks in Europe last summer on my leave. It was something I always wanted to do, but my wife and I had never had the money, back when we were younger and raising kids. Now I make sure I have enough to spoil my grandkids and I use the rest to do what I want."

"Sounds like a good approach. I wouldn't mind taking a trip like that sometime." He remembered someone saying Colt was widowed, but the man rarely revealed his personal side.

"It seems like you might have some vacation time coming up. With a certain florist, if my hunches are correct."

Rio didn't answer. He was staring at Kayla as she and Jenny moved from groomsman to groomsman, bridesmaid to bridesmaid, checking their flowers. Kayla walked by him and motioned for him to follow her. "Be right back, boss."

He followed her into the house and she faced him. "What's going on?" Her voice was low and it looked as if they could be discussing the weather.

"We're providing some extra security for the mayor." He leaned close to her ear. "Mickey's dead."

Her eyes widened a tiny bit, but she didn't react otherwise. His respect for her was only surpassed by the feeling that had been growing in him since he first saw Kayla at that barn. A once-in-a-lifetime emotion. "Kayla, we need to talk."

"After, of course." She looked at him and he hoped he wasn't just seeing what he wanted to see.

"This risotto is still too firm." Gloria walked into the kitchen, looking around for Veronique.

"No problem, Gloria. It will become tender over the next half hour. When the ceremony is done, it will be perfect." Veronique said "perfect" like "*parfait*," her French accent on full display for any future clients. Kayla tried not to smirk.

Gloria handed Veronique a spoon. "Well, see that it is. I will say the base tastes divine, as always, although maybe you added a bit too much pepper?" She turned toward Sylvia, who'd just walked in. "It's time, Sylvia. We need to get everyone back inside so that we can start the procession." Clearly Gloria was throwing herself into the ceremony wholeheartedly. Was it because she was worried about Mickey and it was a distraction for her?

"I'll see you out there." Rio couldn't kiss Kayla, but he looked at her and hoped his glance made her smolder.

Judging from the flush he saw on her neck, it had.

Kayla and Jenny agreed to stay on opposite sides of the gazebo, on the edges of the structure. Jenny would give the flower girl the basket of petals to start the procession, and Kayla would stand by for any other emergencies.

Looking around, Kayla realized how easy it would be to infiltrate the wedding. *Infiltrate.* She hadn't been with Trail Hikers for a week and she was already thinking like an agent.

After the guests were seated, the string orchestra began to play. The gazebo and yard were very large, but even so, Kayla was astounded that all 250 guests were crammed into a venue of that size. The folding chairs were set close together, and as Cynthia had insisted, everyone fit.

Charles Blackwell looked handsome standing at the altar, albeit far too old for Cynthia. Kayla checked him out, from his grey hair to the formfitting tuxedo on his slim, athletic form. He'd be a catch for the right woman. Not for a conniving witch like Cynthia, though.

Not your concern.

The music swelled as Judge Blackwell's mother was escorted by a man Kayla assumed was his brother, judging from the strong family resemblance. The woman was clearly an octogenarian, but appeared fit and much younger in a chic off-white dress, not the woman who'd been described as in a nursing home and too ill to attend. She hadn't been at the rehearsal dinner and Kayla wondered if they hadn't invited her. Yet another case of Charbonneau manipulation and deceit.

Gloria followed, escorted by a groomsman, a fill-in with Mickey missing.

Not missing. Dead.

Kayla allowed the shudder to pass through her. They had a mission to accomplish and she couldn't afford to allow her emotions to control her.

But you can't control love.

No, she couldn't and she'd take that up with Rio

after they closed this case. Maybe even right after the wedding, if they caught the second suspect before the day was out.

Chapter 20

As Gloria approached the gazebo, she tripped on something unseen in the garden, and a groomsman steadied her. Her face was pale and she looked almost…nauseated. Kayla imagined the emotions of the day were getting to her, and wondered if the mayor had told her about Mickey. It would certainly explain the pained expression on her face.

Gloria was seated in the chair second from the end of the first row of white folding chairs. She was no more than ten feet from Kayla, who remained off to the side in front. As Kayla started to make her way farther back so that she and Jenny could leave the gazebo unnoticed by the guests, Gloria's hands reached upward as she coughed uncontrollably. What was happening? Kayla broke into a run and reached her side just as Gloria collapsed on the wooden gazebo floor.

Her breath was wheezy and her face suddenly puffy. Kayla looked at the groomsman who had escorted Gloria. "Call 911 now." She leaned close to the wheezing woman. "Is this an allergic reaction, Gloria? Do you have an EpiPen?"

Gloria nodded but couldn't speak between painful gasps for breath. Kayla stood up.

"Does anyone have an EpiPen? Is there a doctor here? I think she's going into anaphylactic shock." Gasps and murmurs rolled through the seated guests as two shot up and ran toward them.

"I'm a nurse."

"I'm a PA."

Kayla stepped back and allowed the medical professionals complete access to Gloria. A woman ran forward, holding out an epinephrine injectable. "This is my son's, he's allergic to bees."

"Here!" The nurse held up her hand and gave the pen to the PA, who quickly opened it and stabbed it into Gloria's thigh.

Kayla watched from a few feet away and was aware of Rio and other uniformed officers surrounding the area. The orchestra was off under a separate tent and finally stopped playing, which Kayla took to mean they'd gotten word to halt the proceedings.

"They need to wait." The mayor barked his request but no one paid attention.

"No, don't stop for me. I'm fine." Gloria was struggling to sit up, her breathing more normal and the effects of whatever had triggered her attack fading. "It must have been the risotto."

"Are you allergic to anything besides scallops?" Kayla remembered Gloria specifying to Veronique at their planning session that she couldn't have scallops.

"No, nothing. I've never reacted to anything besides scallops. I tasted the seafood risotto ten minutes ago and I started having symptoms immediately. I thought the tightness and flushing was just nerves."

Kayla knew her mic was picking all of this up and hoped that Rio, with his headpiece that everyone assumed was for security, was sending someone into the kitchen and dining room to look for suspects.

"Put me in my chair until the paramedics get here. As long as I'm getting better, there's no need to change any of this. Keep on with the wedding."

"Maybe this wedding isn't supposed to happen." Charles Blackwell, the handsomest groom Silver Valley had seen in a long while, spoke aloud. "It's all been so rushed. Maybe we've been rash to hurry so much."

"Now, now, let's calm down. That's just wedding jitters talking." Sylvia, the minister for the interdenominational service—via a license she'd obtained on the internet—switched back into assistant mode. "Gloria, you look better. Sit there, and let's keep it going."

The mayor looked less than eager to continue, but Gloria was adamant that they should. Reluctantly, he pointed and nodded at the orchestra.

The violinist stood and started the processional. The baroque melody was haunting in the misty yard. Sunlight was just started to peak through the clouds and Kayla wondered if they'd catch a rainbow.

On cue the flower girl came out of the house, tossing the fresh peach rose petals that Cynthia had insisted upon. *Not pink, not blush, but peach.* She knew what she wanted, that was for sure. Each of the bridesmaids came out on the arm of a groomsman and took their place at the front. The doors were closed after the last bridesmaid made it down the aisle, and the standing crowd waited, looking at the house's back porch.

With a dramatic flourish, the doors were opened by two of the caterers and Cynthia stood at the threshold, the house acting as a backlight for her puffy gown and ridiculous floral tiara. She smiled and started down the porch steps. When she was halfway to the gazebo, the EMTs arrived, rushing toward the guests. Cynthia paused, only a few feet from Kayla.

"What's going on?"

"Gloria is in anaphylactic shock." She purposely didn't mention that Gloria was going to be okay.

Cynthia's eyes widened and a strange yelping sound came out of her mouth. "But we're not having the risotto until after the vows are said."

Kayla allowed a second for Cynthia to realize what she'd said and then moved toward her. As she did, Cynthia took off running toward the front of the house. Kayla was on her heels and easily took down Cynthia, who wore five-inch Jimmy Choo's and had a hell of a lot of fabric to grapple with.

Silk tore as Kayla fought with it as much as with Cynthia. She heard shouts from the other law enforcement, but couldn't wait for their backup before she neutralized Cynthia.

A quick, piercing stab to her side made her wince, but she held on to Cynthia, who was stronger than she looked. She flipped Kayla on her back. "You need to mind your own business. You've been a thorn in my side since Gloria sent you out to the Weddings and More Barn that night."

"It was you." Kayla felt woozy and her side throbbed, but she wanted Cynthia to confess on the feed.

"It's always been me. And it's going to be me. I've got it all planned. Are you dizzy, Kayla? You look really pale."

Black spots started to speck her vision and Kayla was almost grateful for them. Being straddled by a suspect she was supposed to be neutralizing was humiliating. Except for Rio, she had nothing to keep her conscious—

Rio!

"Get. Off. Me." She mustered every last bit of strength she had and reached up for Cynthia's hair, which she grabbed and pulled with all her might. She felt crushed flowers in her palm as she'd managed to get a good portion of the headpiece in with the fistful of hair.

Cynthia's scream was the last thing she heard.

"Gunshot victim. Send EMTs to right side of house, beyond the fountain." Rio spoke as he ran, Colt right behind him. The sight of Kayla lying on the ground with Cynthia Charbonneau on top of her, blood seeping into the white fabric where it touched Kayla's side, was horrifying.

He'd seen blood before. It didn't prepare him to see the woman he loved in mortal danger.

"Get off her!" He reached for Cynthia but Colt grabbed his shoulder and spun him around. Angry, he tried to shove Colt off until he saw Colt's weapon pointed toward Cynthia, his expression grim.

"Drop the knife." Colt issued the warning as he let go of Rio and took a firmer stance. Rio knew Colt was a split second from firing. He aimed his weapon on Cynthia, too, who held an open switchblade in her hand, Kayla's blood dripping from it.

"You heard him, drop it."

"Cynthia, stop! What on earth are you doing?" The mayor and groom had caught up to them and Tony was trying to get his daughter to look at him. "Drop it, honey. Listen to them."

Rio didn't give a crap about anything but getting to Kayla. He had to get Cynthia off her before she bled out. But if they messed this up, Cynthia could deliver a fatal blow to Kayla if she hadn't already.

The mayor walked closer to his daughter.

"Stop right there, Tony. We'll take you both out if we have to." Colt's voice was steady and there was deadly force in his tone.

The mayor froze.

"Cynthia, please, drop the knife."

She looked up from Kayla's pale face, growing paler by the moment. "I did it for us, Daddy. You and me. We're a team. We're going all the way."

"You did what for us, Cynthia?"

"It was only supposed to be Meredith, when we found out she knew too much. You think Mickey was going to take care of her? No, he wasn't. He was afraid of going too far, of hurting her too much if he lost his temper. And then you know what, Daddy? He was having an affair with Gloria. She was screwing your best friend. I wanted to tell you sooner and he said if I did he'd tell you I killed Meredith. So I killed him, Daddy, and Gloria would be out of the picture, too, if she hadn't had to shove that risotto in her mouth before she was supposed to." Cynthia's face was flushed and bore the markings of someone who had lost all touch with reality. Rio had seen it before.

"Put the weapon down, Cynthia." He gave his last warning, knowing that he'd take her out with no regret if she moved the knife anywhere near Kayla.

Cynthia looked at her father, then briefly at Charles. "We were supposed to have the perfect marriage." She smiled, a sick, twisted smile. Looking at Rio and Colt, she lifted the knife in front of her. "If you think I'm going to let myself go to prison for the rest of my life, guess again." A gunshot rang out as Detective Bryce Campbell, serving backup for today's op, shot the knife out of her hands just as she turned it toward herself. Cynthia started screaming and within two seconds SVPD officers had her cuffed and facedown on the lawn. EMTs rushed in to aid Kayla, but Rio reached her first.

"Sir, we need complete access."

"Kayla, can you hear me?" She didn't stir and he

reached for her wrist, but was pulled off by Colt before he got in the way of the EMTs. "Rio. You have to let them work."

He stood, never taking his eyes from Kayla. She had to make it. The ground near her was soaked with a puddle of blood, but he couldn't—wouldn't—accept that it was enough to kill her.

He hadn't told her he loved her yet. Hadn't convinced her to lower those strong defenses of hers, convinced her that he'd be there for her no matter what.

The medics worked on her and loaded her onto a stretcher.

"They've got a life-flight helicopter landing now," said Colt, his hand on his earpiece. "It's in the baseball field at the end of the block." As the medics rushed Kayla toward the helicopter, a cold shroud covered Rio's heart. His love for Kayla hadn't been enough to keep her safe today.

Kayla hadn't ever had surgery before. She'd never experienced the disorientation of narcotics. Her mouth was dry and she felt very, very shaky. The attending trauma surgeon had told her she was lucky in that while Cynthia had hit an artery, she'd only nicked it. No major organs were injured, just some deep-tissue trauma to the surrounding muscles. The doctor had assured her that she'd get stronger each day.

"You need to rest. You'll come home with us and I'll make you chicken soup." Her mother and father smiled at her on either side of her bed, having come back from their sales jaunt in Europe at about the same time she'd been shot.

"That's okay, Mom. We can order out." Keith chuckled from the side chair where he'd stayed, playing with his tablet to give their parents room to fawn over her.

"My chicken soup is fine. What's the problem?" Mom never understood that their only memory of her cooking in their childhood was chicken soup. They'd had a constant string of nannies and housekeepers overseas while serving with the Foreign Service, so she'd never branched out much in her cooking.

"No problem, Mom. I'll eat whatever you give me. Has anyone else been by, while I've been in here?" She knew she'd been admitted yesterday; the wedding that never happened was Saturday, so she knew it was Sunday now.

No Rio.

"No, honey. Your police friend—" she looked at Keith "—what was his name?"

"Rio Ortega." Keith's grin was annoying. No amount of painkillers could make her brother's teasing anything less.

"Yes, Rio. He stayed at your side for the entire time you were out. Waited through your surgery, then in here. Once you started to stir, he left. That's what the nurses told us. They'd asked us to go home last night, to get rest, and he said he'd stay here with you."

A memory popped in her mind. Rio's scent, a kiss on her forehead, a soft statement.

I'm sorry, he'd said.

What was he sorry for?

"Oh, wait, there was someone else. A nice woman with silver hair named Claudia came by earlier today. She left those flowers over there for you." Keith held up a huge bouquet of pink peonies for her to see. "They're from Kayla's Blooms, by the way."

"They're beautiful. Jenny outdid herself." She longed to be back in her shop, her nose in flowers. Anything besides lying here, waiting to heal.

Waiting for Rio.

Chapter 21

"Rio, where do you want me to put these files?" Nika stood in front of his desk.

"Here, I'll take them."

"You should have more time for them now, right? Are you wrapping up the Charbonneau case soon?"

"Yes, I'm writing my closing notes on it now, and then all I'll have left is to testify in court." At which he expected Cynthia Charbonneau to be put away for life, be it in prison or a mental lockdown facility after murdering two people, Meredith and Mickey, and attempting to kill Kayla and Gloria.

"You did a great job getting Cynthia's full confession."

"She's like every other sociopath. They always want you to know how smart they are."

"How's Kayla?" Nika stared at him.

"She's better. At home." At her place, since it was safe for her to go home now. He'd missed her presence in his house.

"Have you seen her lately?"

He tried to muster a glare at Nika to remind her that it was none of her business. He failed.

"No. I've been busy wrapping this up."

Nika stared at him a moment longer.

"Don't wait too long, Detective."

"Thanks, I'll keep that in mind. How's your training going, Nika?"

"I knew you had something interesting going off in your off-hours. I had no idea how much it involved, however." Nika was the newest recruit to the Trail Hikers.

"You'll be glad for the training when you have to go into Silver Valley High School undercover."

"Yes, I will. And it will be my pleasure to bring down those loser drug dealers as soon as I find them, believe me."

He suspected the drug dealers Nika was going in to root out would end up being connected to the True Believers. All of Silver Valley's recent problems seemed to lead back to them. But he wasn't working that case.

"Thanks again for your support, Rio. I know I wouldn't be in TH without your recommendation."

"You've earned it, Nika." The use of first names indicated they were both on the same team and same level when it came to the secret agency.

"See you." She walked off and he stood up from his desk. His restlessness was getting the best of him.

More like Kayla had gotten the best of him. *All* of him.

He'd been unable to get Kayla off his mind since he'd made sure she'd survived Cynthia's attack.

Cynthia had tried to kill Kayla before the wedding, too. He'd gotten the confession from her during questioning. She'd been the one who'd fired at Kayla in the parking lot a week before the wedding. She'd seen Kayla's van at the end of the drive by the Weddings and More Barn and had suspected that Kayla had witnessed Meredith Houseman's final minutes.

And then she'd admitted to killing Mickey, claiming it was because she was angry at him for having an affair with Gloria. She'd gone on to brag about putting the scallops in the risotto after Veronique had finished cooking it. Solely for Gloria's benefit.

Obtaining the confession had been satisfying, but Rio couldn't forget how helpless he'd felt as he watched Kayla lying on the grass, bleeding and unconscious. He hadn't gotten to her fast enough, and she'd gotten hurt.

After all his attempts to show her that unlike the places she'd lived growing up, the friends she'd made, that he wasn't going anywhere, that she could count on him, he'd failed her. He'd left her, too.

His cell phone vibrated.

Claudia.

"Rio. Can you meet me in Colt's office in five?"

"Will do." He finished up the last paragraph on the

report and clicked Save. He thought he'd have more of a feeling of satisfaction than he did at the moment.

Claudia was already in Colt's office, seated in one of the chairs in front of his desk. Rio nodded to Colt and her.

"Good morning."

"Have a seat, Rio." Colt sipped his coffee, his expression relaxed.

Why did it feel as if he was about to be chastised?

"Colt tells me that you haven't spoken to Kayla since she's been home, Rio. It's been two weeks. She's going back to work at the shop tomorrow."

"That's great news. She's a tough woman."

Colt and Claudia exchanged a glance that made Rio go cold.

"Is this a meeting to tell me how to run my personal business? I'm an SVPD detective and a Trail Hiker, but my personal life is mine."

"To a point, yes." Claudia shifted in her seat so that she could face Rio head-on. "Your well-being is definitely our concern, as is any Trail Hiker's. Kayla and you need each other, Rio. Tell me you don't already know that."

"I know I need her, but she doesn't need me, not if I can't be there for her in her time of need."

"You were there for her. Knock off the martyrdom, Rio. We were all there. The actions of a murderer are never predictable. Have you thought about that?"

Rio gritted his teeth and counted to five before he responded.

"I should have stopped the entire mess."

"Nonsense." Claudia picked at something on her pant leg. "You're not giving Kayla any credit here, Rio. She's a trained Trail Hiker, even if she's a novice, and she knew how to handle Cynthia. She kept herself alive."

"We can argue about this all day." Colt cleared his throat. "You know I'm not one for getting too personal, but I'm going to tell you this, Rio. If you don't go after Kayla now, before she gets so pissed off at you for not being there these past two weeks, you'll regret it down the road. If not sooner."

Claudia's eyes were filled with concern, but also… was that amusement? At his angst?

"Colt's right. It's time for you to take a breather, Detective Ortega. Take a week and get some R & R. Maybe think about taking Kayla with you. She's only going to work part-time at the shop for the first few weeks, and I'm sure she could be convinced to get some relaxation herself."

He looked at Claudia, then Colt. Neither budged and their expressions remained neutral. Maybe a little bit encouraging.

"Fine." He stood up. "I'll take a week off. But I can't promise anything else."

Kayla stopped to catch her breath at the workbench in the back room. She'd hired another assistant and a delivery person with Jenny's help. Miranda was learning the front register this morning under Jenny's careful eye.

It felt a bit unbelievable that she'd been working as

a Trail Hiker agent at the Charbonneau wedding only two weeks ago.

The bucket of peonies at her feet reminded her of the flowers Claudia had sent while she was in the hospital.

Her side still ached where the knife had pierced through the Kevlar and resulted in a collapsed lung.

She turned to get Jenny or Miranda and almost slammed into a large man. It was the best pain she'd felt in weeks.

Rio.

"Hi, Kayla."

"Will you ever not sneak up on me?"

"Jenny let me back here."

She looked at him, careful not to meet his eyes right away. He was the same and smelled the same. As she gathered the courage to meet his eyes, she saw something she'd never noticed in him before. Uncertainty.

"What do you want, Rio?"

"I was hoping I'd catch you on a break or even lunch. We need to talk."

"You could have called." Irritation trickled into her awareness of him. "A week ago, or better, two, you could've called. Or come over to my house and talked to me. I was pretty much stuck on the sofa, watching *NCIS* reruns with my parents."

"I met them." His eyes had a strange light. "They're very nice. And very devoted to you."

She shrugged. "Whatever."

He rocked back on his heels, his hands in his pockets. "Can I take you to lunch?"

"What's the point? Do you want to hash out the details of the case, for closure? I already did that with Claudia." Of course he knew that, she was certain. "You'll be relieved I don't have to do another Trail Hikers mission—" she lowered her voice "—unless I want to."

"Do you?"

"Yes," she replied without hesitation.

He gave her a slow once-over, leaving no inch of her unexposed to his sexy stare. She'd missed him so much when he'd cut off communication these past two weeks. He hadn't answered her texts or visited, except for the hospital vigil that had made him sainted to her family.

It was no use. She was still hot for Rio.

"What?" She wiped her brow with her gloved hand and attempted an insouciant stance.

"Come to lunch with me."

She took off her gloves slowly. Why make it easy for him? "Fine."

He drove them to a local park that was known for its magnificent views of the valley and Appalachian Mountains that surrounded them. They walked a short distance to a picnic table, Rio carrying a cooler.

"Did you pack a lunch for us?" She was impressed with his forethought, but didn't want to give him the satisfaction of saying so.

"I did. But we're going to do something fun, Kayla. I think we've both learned how short life can be." As soon as she was seated on the bench next to him, he opened the cooler and pulled out two bowls, into which he scooped vanilla ice cream, then sprinkled some nuts and topped it all with canned whipped cream.

"Those look delicious. Who needs lunch?"

"Wait. We're missing the best part." He took a thermos out of the other bag he'd had slung over his shoulder and poured hot fudge over their concoctions.

"You did this all yourself?" She didn't mean to sound so doubtful of his culinary skills, but the only skills of Rio's that she'd seen in action were lovemaking and law enforcing.

"Why are you blushing?" His low voice was gentle, and when he touched her cheek she blinked back a tear.

"I hardly know you."

"I know, and that's going to change. Consider this our first date."

"Haven't we kind of fast-forwarded through that already?" Was he thinking they weren't going to make love again until they knew each other better?

"Some parts, yes. Other parts, we could use some catching up. I want to know why you chose flowers for a living, why you've stayed in Silver Valley apart from the fact that you didn't want to move around anymore. I want to know how it is a local boy like me has fallen for an international girl. I want to know what kind of wedding you want and how many of my kids you're willing to have. If any." He grinned and dug into his sundae.

She couldn't think of eating her ice cream. Not yet.

"Did you just say…"

"I did. I want to spend the rest of my life with you, Kayla. I couldn't come here sooner, come to you earlier, because I had to get over my stupid pride." His eyes grew somber and her stomach flipped. "When I saw you lying on the ground, maybe bleeding out, I felt as if I'd failed you on so many levels. I never want to feel that way again. I love you, Kayla, and I'll wait as long as it takes to convince you that we belong together."

She couldn't see him very well as his face shimmered through her tears.

"I love you, Rio. I wanted to tell you after the wedding. I thought we'd have time. And then when I blacked out, I was certain I'd missed my chance. That we'd had the only chance we were going to have."

He put down his spoon and drew her close to him, caressing her jaw with his fingers. "We've got this chance, Kayla, and I'm not going to let it escape me. I love you, darling." He kissed her then, and it was so tender it released something in Kayla and more tears slid down her cheeks. Rio's rough fingers wiped her face and he smiled against her lips. "Don't cry, babe. This is our happy ending."

She laughed and for the first time in two weeks, it didn't hurt.

"It'll never end for us, Rio. This is where we start." She kissed him. "Together."

* * * * *

REQUEST YOUR FREE BOOKS!
2 FREE NOVELS PLUS 2 FREE GIFTS!

H HARLEQUIN®

ROMANTIC suspense

Sparked by danger, fueled by passion

HRS15

He could see Annabel wanted to ask him more. She might
be a police officer, but she had questions like a detective.
"You can't blame yourself for the decisions your mother
made. I used to think I must have done something to make
Matthew Colton unhappy at home. I tried to connect my
actions as a child to his actions as an adult. They aren't
related. Whatever you did when you were a boy and
however that affects Regina, that's hers to deal with."

He liked what she was saying. Logically, he understood
that he couldn't have done anything different to help
Regina, but emotionally, it was hard to let go of the past.
"Thanks for saying that." It unburdened his soul, though
not entirely. Nothing could fully absolve him of the guilt
he carried.

"Sure." She tossed the bread she'd been using in the
trash and then walked slowly to the front door, grabbing
her coffee-stained pants. She spun on her toes to face
him. "I still owe you a cup of coffee."

He had long forgiven her, but he wouldn't turn down the opportunity to see her again. "Maybe next time I'm in town, I'll stop by the precinct and see if you're available."

"I'd like that."

He crossed to the door. He had manners; he would open it for her. Annabel was living up to that first impression he'd had of her. She was gorgeous, obviously, but she was thoughtful and classy and smart. How was this woman not already taken? Maybe she was as messed up as he was in relationships. Devastating childhoods left their mark, and that mark was often ugly and deep.

Their hands brushed, and electricity snapped between them. The air around them heated and sparked. She backed up against the door.

Her palms were flat against the door and her mouth was tipped up invitingly. He set his hand on her chin, lightly, testing her reaction. He was aching to kiss her, and his palms itched to touch her. Did she want this, too?

Don't miss
COLTON'S TEXAS STAKEOUT by C.J. Miller,
available April 2016 wherever
Harlequin® Romantic Suspense
books and ebooks are sold.

www.Harlequin.com

HARLEQUIN®

A *Romance* FOR EVERY MOOD™

JUST CAN'T GET ENOUGH?

Join our social communities
and talk to us online.

You will have access to the latest
news on upcoming titles and special
promotions, but most importantly,
you can talk to other fans about your
favorite Harlequin reads.

Harlequin.com/Community

 Facebook.com/HarlequinBooks

Twitter.com/HarlequinBooks

Pinterest.com/HarlequinBooks

THE WORLD IS BETTER WITH

Romance

Harlequin has everything from contemporary, passionate and heartwarming to suspenseful and inspirational stories.

Whatever your mood, we have a romance just for you!